Tripping Balls

Goeni Schindler

HellBound Books Publishing LLC

Tripping Balls

A HellBound Books LLC Publication

Copyright © 2017 by HellBound Books Publishing LLC
All Rights Reserved
2nd Edition

Cover and art design by G. Schindler/HellBound Books

No part of this book may be reproduced, stored in a retrieval system, or transmitted by any means, electronic, mechanical, photocopying, recording or otherwise without written permission from the author This book is a work of fiction. Names, characters, places and incidents are entirely fictitious or are used fictitiously and any resemblance to actual persons, living or dead, events or locales is purely coincidental.

www.hellboundbookspublishing.com

Printed in the United States of America

Gocni Schindler

Tripping Balls

A HellBound Books Publishing LLC Book
Houston TX

Tripping Balls

This Work of fiction is intended for Mature audience

Tripping Balls

Dedications

This book is dedicated to the bullshit in life.
The derelict never feeling a part of something
To those, who wondered down long halls of school, always on the outside of cool
Those receiving an ass beating, either physically, mentally or both
For those who love with their all, uniquely born, never finding home
Ones who attempted to do, yet, continually get knocked down
To you little dreamers, sitting, listening to your heart, instead of some ass holes' brain washing
To all the masses, that were deceived, sitting in a church pew
To the neighborhood weakling, who finally said enough
Bikers who ride to die free
Americans that respect the land
Veterans that are left to rot on a street curb
For the slave that works for minimal pay
Grandmothers People, Cherokee Nation
Ones who never quit, laughing at being told no.
Convicts that turned their life around
The ones who live in a place they don't belong
IT Contractors, who never find their place
My mom, who gave me life, thanks a lot
Natives, that got screwed by fool's love for gold
To those who still believe in America
My Best friend, who picked me up off the street
Marijuana, nature's cure all to life

Tripping Balls

Contents

Dedications	7
HELL-A-EXPENSE	15
The Grove	31
Broke Ass City Bus	33
JACKET	37
LoSt	39
Cost	43
The Rambler	47
Johnny B Fast	49
HEAD	52
Driver, Oh, Bus Driver	54
I NEED A CIGARETTE	57
Henrietta, What a Bitch	60
Better Writer	71
Mental Blues	73
HOBO'S LOST PARADE	80
IN LIKES WITH LUCIFER	82
Oliver	85
The Great American Con Job	86
PARADISE	88
TIME IS NOT OUR FRIEND	99
Bad Management	101
THE MANDATE	111
CHILD	116
For You	117
Be the clown, not the cow	120
Machine	121
Wanted Invisible	123
Whimpering Complaint	125
Fully Cooked	127
Meet Sara and Dave	129

patience for the laugh	131
Little Being	135
SANITY VIA CRITIQUES	138
CAPTAIN ASS HAT	141
3:13	156
John Smith	157
SLEEP	160
Old in the Rain	165
Kaboooooom	170
JOURNEY WITH ME	172
S-12 A-16 M-08	177
Something Nice	179
MOTHER	180
WORLD OF MAKE BELIEVE	183
Walking into Oblivion	187
I WON THE LOTTO	190
Living on Empty	192
Dear Zombies	194
LOST IT ALL	195
WHAT IF	199
EVIL	200
ADVERTISEMENT	202
WEEK OLD CHICKEN DINNER	203
THE ACT	206
THE GREAT ILLUSION	208
Welcome to the World	210
Complacency, Your Dead End	213
RAPED NATIVE FOLK	214
Unilluminated	216
Diary of the Non-Influential Man	217
HUMANITY O'HUMANITY	218
TEN to ONE	222

BLACK HAIR	225
Green Rain	226
Meet Dick and Jane	228
THE TALE	229
PRISON	235
Actor Man	242
SAVE THE DAY	248
BAD DAY	250
END	253
Safe Place, it's Five AM	255
A BIG THANK YOU	262
Author Bio	263
Other HellBound Poetry Titles	265

Tripping Balls

Gocni Schindler

Life is a disaster that happened accidentally

Tripping Balls

HELL-A-EXPENSE

Oh goody, what's this?
Hooray, finally, some company
Hey great, glad you made it
We want to take you on a little trip
Possession, that is!
So, buckle up compatriot
Going to be one HELL-A-RIDE
It's time
Us, in this guy
Sitting in He-man underoos
Damn this boobtube
This guy
Too broke to have a 55"
Humans, walking these out the store on the daily
Lame ass, get a credit card
Oh goody, look at this here
Wonderful, the news
Money for the monkeys
Marketing is what we need
This evil makes us proud
Sexy, look at you
Feel that rodents
It isn't a hand out
Greed, it's mine though
Now you can't afford
Anything at all
Like a broke ass song
The rich though, we influence them all
Purchase the world they think
Go in with big coins
With mighty paper, worth
Buy it all

Tripping Balls

One hundred new best friends
Super happy days, everyone loves them
Salesmen, come out of the wood work
White pearly smiles
Happy words to sap an ear
Not for the new toy
No way!
Not because he got you a deal
Hell no!
But for feeding his broke ass soul
Never poor
Commission livings
A tough go
Except for the guy on a podium
YOU DIDN'T KNOW!
Sweet baby Jesus, pay attention
momma's gotta love
Check it out
Go diamonds, those motivational speakers
Go preachers of the word, redeemer
Its dollar bills they serve
Go Politicians
Lining their pockets
Obviously at someone else's
Hell-A-Expense
Sell another positive book
Hey you, did god tell you to write that?
Broke asses gotta give the tithe
Reach deep, in the pocket
That is ten percent
HELL-A-EXPENSE
On the
LIFESTYLES OF THE RICH AND GREEDY!
Loving our influence with that
Give a donation

Healing your ass pits
Oh damn
What's that?
6 months later, another corpse
Parasite in an open pit
Wait for it, another excuse
Speaking of that
"So, what is your excuse?"
Suddenly, HALLELUJAH god came to you
Some cunt in a white beanie, call it Miracle
HERE IS THE NEW BOOK for Hell-A-Expense
Prophecy after all
Shit, TV is such a bore
Isn't that cute
Human parasites doing a dance
"What did you do with the remote?"
Douche shoved it in the back of the chair
Thankfully though, we can now flick the channel
Oh splendid
A shopping show, some stupid shit
Lonely granny, to buy with a credit card
This garbage is lame
We need a cheap whore
What to do, what to do?
We know, off to a human Box Store
"Remember, this is all your fault!"
Flip the switch
Get this body a stepping
Out the front door
Aimlessly looking
Need to borrow
Oh look, a midsize 4 door
Spare key under the driver's door
Yes, always like that
Love those handy magnetic boxes

Tripping Balls

Full tank of gas, thanks for that
Drive, drive, drive
To the Box we go, in this new borrowed ride
"No, we never steal!"
While shopping for bigger, better, more
Products, from CHINA-EXPRESS
Get it cheap
Get it HOT
Luckily for us, the Chinese have suicide nets
These fuckers need to work
America's new slave, Chink's that is
"You can't say that! Is that what you said?"
"What's that? Racism."
"Fuck you, happen to be a demon, doing what we want!"
Chink stuff is what we said
"Don't get all prissy in the pants"
"Bitch, your house is full of it!"
Need to have the product
Want to have it now
Park the car and into the BOX store
Right there on an end cap
"Hey you, grab a pair of scissors."
Shits made in China, better take two
Aimlessly walking
Back of the store
Eyes locked at printers
Take it out of the packaging
Testing, gotta verify
Chinamen got it right
Shit has got to work
USB sold separately
Cheap ass holes
Ten bucks! What's up with that?
Screw you middle man

Just need to get it out
The scissors, snap in half, damn the luck
Made in China, no shit
Good for us, we grabbed an extra
"What is that you say?"
"Laptop, On Display"
"You're kinda a useful parasite, now aren't ya?"
Connect the printer
Garbage auto installs
Fucking BEAUTIFUL things
Open a package of paper
Six dolla and change,
Criminals, taking it to the bank
Unions have bills to pay
Insert a quarter of the bundle
Drop the rest
It beautifully floats all over the floor
Making a wonderful mess
We're an artist after all
Call it, Le Ingenuity of Hell-A-Expense
Who doesn't love Celine, that French guy?
Maybe we meant Fry, pondering
To Hell with it, not like you care
Like anyone gives a rip.
"Are we right or I AM right?"
"Just shake your head for yes parasite, thank you!"
PHOTO PRINT
These cartridges
HELL-A-EXPENSE
Open the package
Toss up the maintenance lid
Remove some blue tape
CLICK, CLICK, CLOSE LID
Test page, ugh, thanks again
Printer Manufacturer

Tripping Balls

WASTING US, SOME PRECIOUS INK
Crooked bastards, screwing us to a wall
Not quite like Jesus
More like Jesus, the lawnmower guy
Mexican's get a bad rap
Flip the lid, its scanner time
This guy's crispy dollar bill
Make us some copies
COLORED COPIES THAT IS
Double sided print
Hundreds of them
With the scissors
Its snip, snip, snip
Fake dolla bills
Filling these pants
Wanting to feel the stripper essence
Rubbing these balls with crisp new dolla bills.
ENTER EMPLOYEE OF THE MONTH
A little bitch named Tim. Scrawny little guy with danger in his eyes. Someone who obviously belongs to the Mormon church. Yet, we all now, is still sucking from the tit.
Tim
"AHEM, Sir! What's going on here?"

Paying no mind to the voices, have enough of those inside this guy's head and besides, we have things to do, like printing dolla bills from this printer. Reluctantly to give a rip, we do our best to answer

Demon
"Testing the printer parasite!"

In an annoying, yet, shocking tone, because apparently, he doesn't know who he's addressing and, wants to grow a pair. Must have been in one of those, manager associate meetings. The kind, where the manager dictates just how importantly insignificant you really are! Oops, sorry, we meant an important resource to the company. Yeah, that was the slogan they sold him. Be bold or some bullshit

Tim
"Ahh, you'll have to buy these items sir!"
Getting annoyed, turning only to see a freckled nerd twerp with glasses as stated above. With best observation, it's beginning to look as if he just got off the ship, landing back in reality from a month-long trip to a world of piss and shit in mindcraft.

Demon
"Buy that he says, we have a thought, how about, No! See, you're wrong! Chinamart is a no risk facility, we're giving this Cocksucker a test run, don't you have some mindcraft to play or something rodent?"
Removing the print job, continuing the cutting of dolla bills before we were so rudely interrupted. Tim, decides to chuckle a little bit, because suddenly, this is a comedy

Tim
"It's actually called Minecraft; I'm working making sure everyone feels like a guest."

In all annoyance, we just look on. OK, OK, yes, our eyes might have turned red or something, kind of a defect. So yeah, we retort like this

Demon
"You are not working and we don't feel like a guest; you're pestering the customers, which happens to be us. As you can see, we're just minding our own business running this handy print job!"

Tim, who is obviously disturbed by our acts of self-indulgence, loses his shit, rudely cutting us off from my epic rant. Epic we tell you. I think he is bi-polar, so shh! No, we aren't pointing any fingers. Yes, we are pointing to Tim here, but you didn't see that, so don't be a snitch! We got an eye on you, parasite!

Tim
"SIR!! What in the name of the good father do you think you're doing here? You opened paper, printer ink, the printer as well as that cable! Look at this mess, there is paper everywhere! I'm sorry, you need to pay for this. You can't just come into a store and take things out of their packages and start using them!"

STOP!
Did you read that? What in the name of the good father line! Let me tell you, we've been around for thousands of years and well, yeah, no one has ever said something like that to us before. Kinda awesome don't you think? Correct! "It doesn't matter what you think! Parasites should be seen and not heard"
Now, not really giving a shit what Tim says, for obvious reasons mentioned above! We just courteously respond
Demon
"You should go blow the good father!"

Tim is in a world of confusion but we are a demon after all and have that effect on whimpering little parasites, he probably thinks Joe blow Smith is going to appear and save the day. "Shit, are we in Utah?"
Tim
"Sir, if you don't pay for this, it's stealing and I'm going to call security!"
Thinking as we often do, did this little bastard just accuse us of stealing? Thinking he did! That sure isn't nice. This is where we draw the damn line. A lot of things we are, but a thief isn't one of them. We borrow things, never steal them. Unfortunately, our eyes turn yellow when mad. Occasionally some smoke may potentially billow from our happy hosts mouth and nose, also, we cause our host to fart, a lot, it's terrible. Can barely handle the smell. It's the workings of some real Hollywood special effects here and our host's ass just stinks! Probably should take this body in for a number two. Like an oil change. "What are you doing? Why you trying to smell our ass pervert? Believe the nerve on this one!"

Demon
"Stealing, you kidding me! Now kid, do you see us leaving with this shit from the Chinks? No, just making sure it would work for what we needed and well, it obviously doesn't! What kind of shit are you selling here?
Taking the printed dollar bill in both hands, we show the human filth what it looks like.
Demon
"Look at this shit, does this dollar bill look real to you? With the stupidest look on his face in the history of man he murmurs
Tim

"No, it doesn't sir!"
Demon
"Damn right it doesn't. How are we supposed to pass this off as real to a stripper?"
Having enough of this we spit in his face
Tim sits there with his mouth open as a river of drool hits the floor. The ass hole pissed his pants too. To help him out we stuff the printed dollar bill in his mouth to stop the drool and put some paper clippings to help absorb the liquid coming from his pants leg. Don't look at us like that. Hey, that stuff on the floor could have been a slip and fall accident waiting to happen. Did you know, that Slips, Trips and falls account for 20 percent of all work-related injuries and 5 percent account for fatalities! I know, who knew! Well we did of course. So, us, the GOOD GUY's. Actually, doing this kid a favor here and the Corporation, look at the money they're saving in litigation. We should be getting a paycheck for the services. Don't you think? That's right, it doesn't matter what you think Parasites. You're catching on quick.
Demon
"Got nothing to say for yourself punk! Be thankful I'm in a good mood today and have places to be or I'd be talking to your Manager on your lousy people skills and obvious, lack of customer service! Bitch, you can keep the dollar too!"
Back to the action
Open the lid, grab the crispy dolla bill
Hit the bricks running
Off to the strip club
Porn is free tonight!
Via fake GW's
Thanks' Chinamart for your support
Paper money

Fake money,
"We know what you're thinking!"
"Criminal, right?"
"Kiss us under the bridge in moonlight!"
But hey, like what
She going to start ink testing?
Spreading her legs
Showing her tits
Bust out a yellow pen?
We don't think so; you don't think so!
Glad you're back on the team
Land of the fake
Land of the illusions
Land of Business as usual
Single moms gotta pay rent too
Drive, drive and yes, we drive
Recklessly drive into the fun centers parking lot
It's up over the curb
Slam on the brakes
Whip the car in circles
Good the hell enough
It's out the car running
$10.00 charge at the door
Fucking crooks
$10.00 for a beer
Bastards, not even a reach around
The last $20 bucks this guy had
Now there went the lap dance
Sitting itself down at the stage, front row
It's not a Heavy Metal show
Way better than that
Some fat bald announcer playing DJ
States the name of the dancer
"FYI, His job is comparative to coming back as a
Female/Male bicycle seat, depending on your

preference, something to wish for on the return visit. You can thank us later!"
The Dancer is "Raven the Red"
Oh Goody, we like red, is it Christmas again?
Oh dear, did we say that out loud?
Shit, that will get the Christians all up in arms
Probably come to do an exorcism
We call that, fitness
Dig in the hosts pants, pull out a handful of you know what
"What are you looking at?"
"Don't play dumb, we watched you."
"Oh, you wanted to see this guy's love gun?
"Naughty little parasites, you're going to hell!"
The paper cut on the shaft, well worth it
Here comes the action
She does her sleazy slut dance.
Its once, then twice, three times around the pole
Then the back door shot and the upside down spread
Spin and spin and spin
We bite our host's fist
its stopping us from committing rape again
"You don't judge!"
It's all nice and tight, the way it should be
The way we like it
She makes her way, time to shove the melons in the face
Her essence is of cotton candy with fairy excretion
Making us want to jiz
She looks us in the eyes, smiles, then she opens her mouth
"Lean back baby!"
The voice of a nice little prostitute devil, just for us
Shoving her 9" stiletto into our hosts chest
Sexy long leg pushes us back, hard
We like it rough

She is doing the splits
This guy is hard as a rock
Then suddenly, she is on top of me, we mean us.
"Oh, we see, now you want in on this?"
"Suddenly gotta share this stuff?"
"Stop talking to us, she is looking at us
Like we're fucking crazy!"
We are getting that odd look
Be calm
"Who you talking to baby?"
"Great, now look at what you did"
"If we get kicked out, I'm kicking your ass, parasite!"
She climbs us like we're a rock
Her love muffin is by our mouth
Smells like fresh strawberry, yum, yum's
Dropping onto this guy's man pipe
Yeah, she can tell, wink, wink, its huge at this point
An elegant pierced nipple runs along the side of our nose
Of course, we accidentally give it a lick
She gives us a disgusted look
It was an accident, come on.
I think we're going to get throat punched!
Hell yes, we want it rough!
We wink at her and usher her close
Whisper into her ear
"Don't worry baby, extra for that!"
Blow her a kiss, damn near knocking her off our host's lap
We have that kind of magical effect
She giggles, she shoves her big silicon tits in our face
Suffocating us, literally, can't breathe
No serious, we can't breathe
Fuck, stop, help
Our Host's hands are flapping around for fucks sake

Tripping Balls

The light is going dim
The world ignites in our pants as man shaft explodes
Shoving the fake money in her bikini bottom
She gladly gets off, we kind of all got off
I think she was asking if the shit was real
Not quite sure.
"Did you read anything like that?"
We sure didn't hear anything like that
Then she does the impossible
We can't really believe what is happening
She actually pulls a marker out of her ass
Oh wait, WHAT!
DAMN, SHE DOES AN INK TEST
The world owes
MAKE IT PAY
With crisp new dolla bills
Run, run, run
"Hurry up parasite!"
A big fat bouncer and half naked Raven hot on our tail
Screaming their lungs out
"Stop that guy!"
All this Screaming and shouting from them
Really such a buzz kill.
Come on, you just wanted a little fun
The bullies want to thump a skull, not any old skull
This skull, we happen to be residing in.
"Hey you, just wanted you to know
"I'd really like to trip you! Hahaha"
Laughing as we go
Minds a racing
Let's hope
Security cameras are of no quality
Hell, cameras are black and white's, right?
It's a dark stripper's dirty hole paradise
No problem, we got this

"You're probably wondering why we even care."
"And well, we don't, but let's just roll with it
 as if we did! Shit was your idea, any ol'ways!"
Out the door we go
Jump into the car
Keys in the ignition
Fire it up, Vroom, vroom!
Shut up, it's a four door
It's the only thing we could borrow
Slam it in drive
Floor the gas
One hellacious squeal
Happily, sticking the middle finger out the window
It's off we go!
Driving, driving, driving and yes driving some more
Park the car in some abandoned lot
One block, from our happy host's home
We're not black, just lazy and don't really give a damn
Through the doors, we go
Crawl into bed
Think that was fun
Sleepy time, night, night
Suddenly its
BANG....BANG......BANG at the door
Eyes crack to daylight
Mouth lets out a moan
Our minds ask.......
"What is this? Who the hell is knocking at this guy's door?"
The door is kicked in
What the?!?
THE FBI
Printing dolla bills
Federal Hell-A-Offense
Cause nothing else is

Tripping Balls

There goes the fun
Guns upon thy head
Time to exit
It's been a blast
Possession that is.
The sucker is carried away
Tossed in a cage
"Hope your happy, parasite!"
When a demon appeals to women
It turns out bad
Damn it man
Tits and ass
HELL-A-EXPENSE

The Grove

In the world
From a former age
Bavaria to set the stage
Losing thy way
Searching for something
Uniquely influentially powerful
Selling rightfully yours
Stolen, Humanity in ruins
Taking for granted
Careless, Reckless, Greedy bastards
In a house of sticks
Foundation of bullshit
Remittable ideas
The unit, all destroyed
They came back
Never though, never really left!
Taking yours, giving up rights
Mindless chasing
Paper for worth
Criminals together assembled
Burning before the crotch of an owl
Cloaks to hide
Hideousness so vile
Scared little children
Secrecy in shadows
Fools in wardrobes
Maggots in a closet of palpability
Dickless bishops, worthless rooks
Just pawns on a larger chess board
Distaste upon graces
Just a Bohemian wasteland
Slaves to those who rule
Understanding nothing

Tripping Balls

The rug pulled
All willingly falling
Some fickle childhood nightmare
Illumination of bitches
Men of ill repute
Ruling it all.......society gladly lets them
The Masses mindless fish
It's just, Human beings after all
Disposable to the cause

Gocni Schindler

Broke Ass City Bus

Once upon a time,
on a cold ass winter day
Back in bum fuck no man's land
Broke ass side of Los Angeles
Riding on the city bus
As a broke ass, does!
An elderly man,
with an oversized coat, pays the toll
The moving bus
Wobbles the elderly man
With worn-out knees.
oh, the joy, written on his skin!
Making his way to an open seat.
The bus stops at another bus stop
Receiving more homeless broke ass bums
like the rest of us. Now, on the bus
Colorful array of people; it's really a beautiful sight.
The elderly man, pulling out a brown bag from his
jacket.
Methodically studies it, with a cheery
smile, tosses a couple pills in his hole
Then lifts the brown bag, taking a good long gulp.
It seems to be nothing serious
just something, to take the edge off
Riding the bus can be a living hell
Now, mingling about the bus;
two twenty something punks.
Passing out leaflets, making some
sort of sales pitch.
What a place to sell something.
some Einstein, came up with this plan!
"Let's sell to the broken down,
those without a nickel worth."

Tripping Balls

No wonder stupid people are found in the gym.
Some people are interested; probably
cause they used the term
free, once, maybe twice
Then, some smart
bums are not interested at all!
Note: I love the gym
it's awesome watching people flex in the mirror.
The elderly man doesn't seem to notice, nor give a fuck,
he just makes a frown, while letting out an obnoxious
fart.
The overweight colored gal gives him a dirty look,
Like a trumpet, she sounds off
"OH, MY GOD!"
Picks up her bags and travels to another open spot!
Because, we all know, moving to another part of this
death trap, will make everything, alright!
The elderly man takes another long swig
then looks down to correctly place the brown bag
back in his jacket where it came
A professional drunk who holsters his liquid gun!
As he looks back up,
sure enough; those two twenty something
youngsters are standing over him,
the one is handing him a leaflet.
One wrinkled, shaking hand lays hold
Vintage eyes gazing upon it
Gives a smirk that makes his
wrinkled face look more like that of a pug.
It is almost like a circus
He tosses the leaflet on the ground
"NOW BEGINS THE PITCH."
Listening to the spiel
they attempt to explain, that for a small fee
he too, can get fit like they are

With the help of some bullshit protein drink.
While the other punk reiterates what the first one said!
Now, my thought is "WHY?"
Only $299.00, for only 299.
Why is it always described as ONLY?
Fuckers seem to have forgotten where they are
Shit, that's a years' worth of bus fares
The elderly man takes out the brown bag from his pocket
while murmuring under his breath
Placing the bottle of magic fluid to his lips,
gulping down a bigger swig.
Surely to dull the pain from a terrible pitch.
Sight though, really making me thirst!
Meanwhile, the two twenty something youngster's
kind of look at each other
You know, in that disbelief form of shock
as they ask mentally in their minds
"Is this old geriatric prick really drinking
from a brown bag on a city bus?"
Obviously, that isn't imaginable after all.
Couple of virgin births just happened
Shit, it was a miracle.
Quick, someone call the Catholic church.
The Nancy handing out the leaflet gets back to the sales
gibberish. The old man lets out one hellacious burp,
literally, it damn near blew out the windows.
It obviously stunk of old man rot!
Hilariously, the kid selling eternal life
steps back a bit, more like, knocked back
his eyes twitching! Suddenly, no more like
miraculously, the kid is back at it.
He starts to explain once again!
Going down the leaflet all the benefits of signing up.
Eating better, daily exercise, it just goes on and on.

Tripping Balls

I really had to admire his tenacious willingness to sell!
SUDDENLY, the elderly man just interrupts loudly, this isn't a
quite loud, oh no, this is balls to the walls loud.
LOUD, so loud, that the bus driver looks back in the rearview!
All the commotion on the broke ass city bus just ceases!
We all just blank stare, as the old man with crazy in his eyes,
fire in his nuts, blares with thunderous vocals
"I'm not doing no damn protein drink bullshit! I'm
drinking this bottle while doing some fucking drugs.
Now you damn whippersnappers, go sell to someone
else. This bottle, along with these pills is how a 76-yr.
old war Vet spends his 299.00 on some life altering
fun!"
The Old man had the final word,
a true cowboy in a concrete war zone
The old man's hand grabs the rope,
sounding the alarm.
The buss pulls over, out the side door he goes!
I watch him as he stumbles about
the doors close
The bus drives back on route
the commotion starts again
as if nothing ever happened.
It's an honor to be old
To no longer give a shit
Bless all our vets
God only knows our government won't

JACKET

One
Jacket wears its man
Many, many, colors
Possessed with absurdity
Blackness is 11, it disguises itself
A jacket wears the man
Billions of people
Mindless blank stares
Looking, Seeking, Needing
Filled with anxiety
Ridicule within separation
Wonderers; soulless devils
Nothing breaking 13
Never to be stained
The jacket, one with man
Color disguises the pain
Favored adaptability
Hide thy light
Society; in its duped state
Knowledgeable patterns programmed
Trying to lock down
Unknown to the known
The jacket with the man
11 to be 33 deaths by flesh
One to lock down, three to decipher
Figure out, mysteries
Never, not ever, left alone
Nor conformed, nor reformed
Everything else, magically controlled
9 to the keeper, the inch is attempted
The jacket, taking away more than owed
Hidden white light
Energy within dumbed down

Tripping Balls

The hidden eye turned off
Water is contaminated
Poison in veins
Everlasting power, lost to ignorance
Thinking upon a blue moon
Eleven are doomed
The Jacket knows, sacred knowledge
Man, dissolved from the world
When seen, thirteen one.

LoSt

Momma's not going to save you now
A boy in the mist
Chained to a boulder
Jumping into the abyss
As a teen, living each day
In carelessness, rebellious ways
Eighteen like a flash
Lawless new adult
Direction, none to be found
The worlds hopeless cause
Knowing no respect
Self-love in the toilet
Flushed away was the soul
Not a care for self, for anyone
Holding no purpose!
A world of evil, world of not following rules
Crime was the cause, obviously fun in the moment
Godless destiny
Men in blue
Pointing 9MM upon rancorous personality
Hands up they stated
Face, smashed into drywall
Handcuffed, dragged, tossed into a squad car!
Away with perversity, away
Heavy was the door they opened
The human cage, slammed shut
The echo rings inside the head
One bed, cold, solid steel
MISERABLE!
Pillow, fabricated from cardboard
Its deserved was stated
Tears rained down cheeks
Laughter upon lips

Tripping Balls

Just getting caught, the remorse
Everyone is innocent
Dots in the ceiling
Counting them over and over again
Time can be misery
Dragged down a hall
Man handled into a chair
Some drunken lawyer
The county Public Pretender he was called
A human gowned in black, white was his skin
Hammer eloquently clutched
With office, bold hands
Dry pale lips uttering eloquent noises
Cacophony the youth never understands!
Thunder was the voice
From the god who knows
Going to the end
Hell, shakes free
Heinous acts
To prison with this filth
Experience life
Another youth lost in a cell
Comparatively a chicken
Head to the log
An axe swings down
The body flops around
A lucid outcome
Soon to be a dinner
Served to nothing innocent
lost in the cage
Everything changed
Lawless mind cast into wickedness
Embraced the loving hands of violence
Respect was earned
By fist, by lock placed into sock

Respect earned
Willingly smashed into brawn
Never back down
Giving, NO QUARTER
Not once, not Ever
Time the enemy of flesh
Slowly ticks along
Out of the box
Changed with Uncertainty
Trapped inside the infant's crib
God help to tear out of this beefcake
The hidden rules from the cage
Always expecting defilement
New fear on life,
Vines of wrath wrapped tight
Choking, Slowly, not quick
Savoring the meal
The chump
Inside an imaginary underworld
Wholly Consumed, given zero shelter
An event, unexpected deeds
Bringing one to the knee
Opening eyes while pinned down
New Kings who rule societies scum
Needs they say, urges to be fulfilled
Hands on the back wanting the reward
Spreading the brown flower
With man's natural hose
Fighting against a mob
Stealing reality, the mind in shackles
The beasts set free
Real world is now seen
Find a way the Toad would say
Every day prior The Queen of Spades
To sanctity for a simple Spider

Tripping Balls

A preparation of a game
For a hopeless tomorrow
Evil takes away an Angel
No beliefs within
A mortal wound slow to heal
Never removed
Humanness love Changed
Lost in a consumption of rage
Madness in new light
Guided in a world of negative signs
Finding the no
No way out from inside
Owned by evil, devil's in the detail
Another possession ripped away
Rent is due, they're wanting to be paid
Man's lusted pleasure, dick in a hole
Not today
Headlong into water that houses shit
Can't breathe, violently flailing arms
Reaching for a Gods hand
Not found inside good Michelangelo's bowl
Eyes, frantically searching the toilet hole
Taking water as air
No help around
Legs shake as hands drop to the ground
In the mist, all is gone
A boy chained to a boulder
Momma's not going to save you now

Cost

I hold ZERO desires for this life
While caring less about material things
In some form of honesty
Probably never will care again
In reflection
I've personally watched
Through hazel colored eyes
Four beautiful beings
Gasp that final breath
The eyes detailed the war within.
One was named Sam, I called him son
I've seen the structure of beliefs fail
A false curtain come tumbling down
Exposing a cardboard cutout of a man
No Royal crown, never nothing
Nothing at all
Just a cardboard cut out
Shadowed behind a holy shroud
I understand the gist of silence
Importance of listening well
I've witnessed courage first hand
While living in a place not fit for rats
Understanding seriousness inside respect
Discerning two of the greatest
Gratitude along with humility
Mixed together for a life of simplicity
I've seen the place of compassion
it's something that should be cherished.
Above everything else, COMPASSION
I know injustice first hand
Personally, lived it more times than I care to count
I've seen children go with out
Learned what a handout is all about

Tripping Balls

Free things make you weak
It's best not to take them
Even if you are down, even if you are out
Better to die than be an indebted slave
I know what a lazy hand produces
While a steady hand gains
I know what fear does to the soul
I've witnessed the world's self-destructive ways
Tolerating what a relationship is
How the core is respect, yet countless give no shits
Respect, with a dash of trust and sex
I've seen someone beg at the altar of god
Beg, with the deepest of tears
Only to die like the doctors said
People make excuses to cope with pain
Showed me logic is still dead
I know what it's like to be violated by a man
To be used by a woman who only cares for self
I found the answer to obtain inner peace
Yet in ignorance, have not walked it
I've spoken in the hidden language
Walked amongst the spirits
They touched my mortal hand, tingles, crawled spine
Recognize what my purpose in life is
Not all about that happiness
Placed my scratch upon the imaginary wall
Like children's imagination
During a rain storm
Chalk on black asphalt
Soon, soon it will be gone
I know what it's like to wash blood off my hands
How words can kill the weakest of men
Taken risks helping to ruin people's dreams
Including self
I've been honest, few times shady

Understanding what one is best
Bringing a peaceful night's rest
I've met the one who denied me
Yet gave me life
He's worthless, still I forgave
I've had a few moments of pureness
That makes me rich
I've owned the shoddiest of cars to glittery new ones
Garbage, purposely designed to fail
I've had the American Dream
In my hands like a potted plant
Till it slipped
The fucker wilted away
In tears, I realized
It's all just an illusion anyways
I achieved a few small titles
Nothing worth mentioning
I understand being homeless by living it
Knowing the despair that keeps you there
I know loss is like a fatal stab in the heart
World sits laughing while the blade gets ripped out
Only thing that makes it through
Is self
I've come to accept that people
Choose to be good or evil
Each and every day, I've gotten over it
I live with a great nonphysical pain
It cut me to the core
Altering me from the path started upon
I know there is no moral code
Just ideas of the monster roaming the floors
I know society will fail, darkness prevails
Humans forget history
I've walked in the great waters
Damn, always cold

Tripping Balls

I know the greatest pain a person can experience
While also how to heal
Mind never forgets, makes blessed
I gained understanding dealing with emotions
Undecided how important they are
I acknowledge that a boy
Needs guidance from a man
Not another boy in man pants
Nor a woman who thinks she can
Humans can't change natural law
She can't!
I lived that
I understand there is only one
One set of footprints in the sand
Mine
I find this life boring
Full of repeats, with unending cycles
Its simple math really
I understand the phrase
Nusquam Esse
Yet I don't really know anything!

The Rambler

Coke in my hand
Death in my head
Listening silent
Just fucking listening
Ears turning red
Inner thoughts, rage
I see, question marks
Must be going insane
Why doesn't this woman shut her yap?
An exclamation pops above my head!
"SHE IS SO ALONE..."
Enough to make; one sick
Never, ever, does she
have someone to address
Don't get it, you know
Never, will I understand
How we can be around the world
Yet Loneliness, the only threshold

From a story of fiction, I always wonder.
What is fact?

Johnny B Fast

It's funny, how easily it is to recall
At his rather young age
How it was when he was a child
Life span, like watching a movie
Always a bottle in his hand
From birth till today
Always a bottle
Bottle, in thy hand
Hit the fast forward then rewind in the mind
Surely didn't have it easy
Yet, it wasn't that bad
Time comes rushing back
When one perceives, what is really taken for granted
Shortly to be forgotten, then forsaken again
As the statement goes
"From nakedness, from darkness, I came kicking,
came screaming! So, it shall be when I leave".
How fitting, enter me laughing
The recollection, how he rushed through childhood
While in reality
How was he to know the speed life goes
"Life's cruel joke everyone has to pay!"
He would blab in a drunken state
His parents tried to forewarn
No one, heeds their parent's words
That it goes, fast, take it slow
Don't drink so much, Johnny
Though, as a child, how was he to really know
He was happy, with a bottle in his hand
Gosh, how he busied himself
With such trivial nonsense
Such worthlessness! A giant conspiracy
Just as long, as he had a bottle in his hand

Tripping Balls

Wasn't enough to pass out with a cigarette
Wanting to burn the house down
No, no, no, just put that bottle in his hand
Now, what was obtained is all not worth a shit
What's it worth any way's always on his lips
'Twas given the last rights to life
"six months"
give or take, a day or two
One should often wonder about the end
Though, surely, one is never considering
What it feels like, to hear the words
your time will draw to an end, when it never really began
Let's describe it as this, while he poured another drink
"Numbness at first, then it seems that the brain gives
a flash back of life, suddenly you realize,
you didn't do shit but drink it away. Cheers!"
Surely, truly, he had the feeling to fight
Though, body too weary
Battle has taken its toll
Lying in bed, with his eyes taped open
Not to miss one moment
With that bottle in his hand
Thinking, reflecting
It seems, it's all he could do
Wishing that life in his body
Could stay just one more day
To relive some part of yesterday
The bottle in his hand
Always shared the bed
Turning, it's just an empty nest
Now, thinking about life.
Pondering, Johnny did
What has it been, he would murmur
"Did I live a life worth anything?"

He sure didn't cure any disease
Nor did he sail a ship across the great seas
He was never a valiant soldier
He did nothing really of vast importance
Record these final moments, he pleaded with me
With another bottle in his hands
He had one way to tell the tale
The tale of a life, not lived
When they pulled that empty bottle of whisky
From his stone, dead hand
He still had the infamous smile
That showed
He just never gave a damn
It was his
"fuck you salute"
To life in death
His parents wept
Parents shouldn't burry a child, the topic spoken
Gave them a hug, made the I'm sorry statement
Remember Johnny, their final goodbye

HEAD

Silent echoing
The place, this head
Home of the brain
That darkened mass of nothings, everything
Where the communication of the body is processed
Thoughts, thinking
Chemicals, balance, action, reaction
Boom, boom, boom
A silent echoing, pulsing, pounding
A wretched place we call the head
Where all thoughts are plotted out
Thoughts of murder, of mayhem
Envy, jealousy; even rage
Goodness is engulfed with flames
The wanting, never ending
Time, gripping like a vise
Squeezing the truth that we are something
That we are amounted
What we hold in our hands
Pound, pound, pound
The temples, pulsing to the bass clef
Agonizing the stress of more
Never ending, wanting, feeding the mind like a parasite
Eyes, those villainous little things
Relying on seeing one way
Betrayers of life
Like a fish, after a shiny lure
The big reaction
Chasing those fancy frivolous ideas
The battle of life
Pleasurable feelings
Bring forth thy shit, place it inside
Feed on flakiness, in utter delight

Be the provender
Always devouring fodder
Like a junkie scrounging
For a fix
Always wanting more
These eyes, fucking betrayers
Sackers of lives
Projected persuasion perceives
Brain feels the need
Chemicals releasing
For that short, little, soaring
Relieving a false stress
Eloquently conceived in the mind
Elevating heightened senses
The want, the prison
Caged to desires
Enslaved, captured
It's real for what is fake
Boom, boom, boom
That was a shot
Pounding, enough to drive insane
Life, the walk, taken so long
Too damn short the distance
Like the blind, walking a block
Stumbling lonely in the dark
Never really knowing where they're going
Just going without living
Without experiencing life
Till ending, then, its fully known
Life inside the mind

Driver, Oh, Bus Driver

Insane, a place for the sane
Sitting on the bus
It's a dirty shame
Being broke
Being without an American dream
Bus driver, are you deranged?
Working long hours
Never enough dough
Working on shitty pay
It's all about the pension
The picture of an island dream
That packaged deal
Meals on wheels' babe
Pull through a fast food chain
Its roughly the same
Insane, a place for the sane
Homeless pricks that stink
Of piss, of shit, all the same
Daily, dealing with the down
With the outs
All at another stop along the way
Anger mixed with rage
It equals Shame
Loss, such disgrace
Another homeless VET
With pain etched on his face
Puke, wiped on his sleeve
from the drunkard's gut brawl
Blood stains on knuckles
Marks on the face
I'm sure, it makes the pain go away
Insane, a place for the sane
Another drunken slut

Gocni Schindler

That cusses
That spits
Yes, that's right
Fall flat on your face
We'll all just sit still in our place
Numbingly, we all look away
Another, another, another
While he drives along the way
Drop off, pick up
It's always the damn same
Makes one wonder
What goes through his brain?
In the world of the insane
Please give your bus driver a TIP
He puts up with all the bullshit.

It was a hot day, the bus stunk, People reeked worse. I just couldn't blame him. He was driving like a madman. The drunk white guy landing on the Hispanic. Over the curb, blowing the red light, maybe two. Flying past few of the scheduled stops. The colored gal, coloring her lips, lipstick up her nose. Busting out her phone. Time to do some filming while saying "Oh, hell no!" But hey, it was a hot day, the bus stunk, People reeked worse. I just couldn't blame him.

I NEED A CIGARETTE

Damn these fits
Walk till my feet bleed
Along the endless streets
I need to fix this nicotine machine
There isn't one dime in my pocket
Not one cigarette in my hand
I feel like some damn rat
Just simply trapped within a nicotine fixation
Nicotine to me, the human test subject
Cheese just dangles at the end of a shotgun barrel
All I want is that cheese
An arm's reach away
Give me that nicotine cheese, PLEASE....
Ready to gnaw my way free from NICOTINE
An impossible feat
Begging, pleading
No one seems to give a damn
They don't know the pain
Out of the blue
Then don't ya know it
As I'm on sunset
The Big BLVD
Another homeless prick comes to me
Smacks me in the arm
Making some killer statement
"Like hey man, you got a cigarette?"
Time for the dance with my raging madness
 "Hey man, for 5 dollars you can have a cigarette!'
 "I don't have 5 dollars! Why charging me 5 dollars?"
 "So, I can go buy a pack and give you one!"
 "Dude, if I had 5 dollars I could get a pack that'd be
like 20 cigs. Why would I only get 1?
 "Exactly! This is what I'm talking about!"

Tripping Balls

"Brah, dude, what you talking about? This makes no
sense; no sense. I want a damn cigarette, brah!"
 "Exactly Fucker, think shit is free or something?
No wonder society is screwed with clowns running around
wanting for nothing! As if this a Dire Straits song"
The bum walks away mumbling
Some shit that didn't make sense
Must be one of those lizard alien breeds
Walking the L.A land
I would like to feel bad
I should feel bad
Not really trying to be the douche
Though, no nicotine
Is raging me bad

Gocni Schindler

In the joint, I knew this guy,
he had no money. He was lazy
and wouldn't take the jobs
offered. Guy would dig through
the ashtrays, pulling the butts
and lighting them up.

Henrietta, What a Bitch

Dreaming, dreaming, dreaming
Moving along
Insignificant little minds
Working, always pushing
Seeing, yet never obtaining
Who has time to give a rip
Snails that slither along
Nowhere, nowhere, destination land
Lost riders, off the edge
Weak bastards, pulled by their feet
Speeding car
Weakness, gets dragged along
Skin, peeled, passionately ripped from flesh
Exposing those corrupted bones
A man rides his tractor
sucking on straw
He was a sinful smoker
Who enjoyed his agony
Till Henrietta condemned him
To her version of hell
Lob off thy nuts
Give a good hobbling
Till the bastard
Just a ball-less
Limping, sack-less son of a bitch
Cars speeds past
Speeding ever so fast
Nods are received
Nods are given
RESPECT!
The mind visualizes
Dragged remains sail past
On cables, no less

Gocni Schindler

The farmer contemplates
How to get things done?
Henrietta, here he comes
Like a mongrel, he marches on
Best grab yourself like you had nuts
Take care, fret not...
Your personal slave is here
For he's coming,
To give you a ride
On steel ribbons
Suits the likes of you
Quite well!
Like old times
With a gag in her mouth
Hands bound
Feet tied; to their pile O' Aids car
Must be a Ford
Whip it out, show the manhood
Piss all over
Mark her your own
Its blown in the wind
For a sack-less man
Sitting in the car
Fire it up
Let the throttle down
Show the machine
You are BOSS!
Hand on the shifter
Vision upon the mirror
Peering intently
Eyes, that see something new
A cross dangling in the air
The mind races
The thought;
"Cancel my membership to the virgin birth!"

Tripping Balls

Rip that cross down
Slam the foot down
Smash the accelerator to the floor
Listen intently as the engine roars
Black smoke
Carbon
From pussy foot driving around
Every time that fat hag told you to slow down
This car
Rage, every time, this car, rage
Nothing but a big complaint
Henrietta squirms on the ground
She doesn't understand
Fear grips her
Her mind
Thoughts race
"This must be a joke; He doesn't have the guts!"
Poor Henrietta
Bitch should have made him a sandwich
He found his nuts
Screwed them back on
Shouldn't have been such a cunt
Now look at you
Demons laughing, shouting
"Just drag this wench!"
His Lips utter
"Worthless hag, cunt of a witch!"
Slam the car in drive
Tires roar with small squeals
Toss that fucking worthless crucifix
Ignore that thud
Henrietta, it's about that time
It's time for
ICE CREAM.
Screams, screams, screams

Gocni Schindler

we all scream for ice cream
Kids line up
To see the show
Some toothless con-man selling snow cones
Five dollars here, five dollars there
It's 'cause of the gas, you know
Each day, every day, twice, three times
It's five bucks, to keep the kids quiet
It's five bucks; three times a day
Snow cones; giving the kids the shits
Who's running the circus?
Toilets comes to life
When a rectum hits the bowl
The bowl begs like a dog
Fill me up; with ex-lax snow cones
Cars drive fast
A mommy looks past
An old man smoking a cigarette
In some pile O'Aids wreck
Give a good old wave
Wave while watching as two stumps
Once called legs
Whip all over the road
Shits all smiles when Mommy waves back
The woman in a hell-bent heat of rage
Thinks of little Timmy
Dumping his intestines
In the famous latrine
Where the sign states
LET'S GO POTTY FOR MOMMY PLEASE!
Mothers; such good little creatures
Always looking out for number ONE
Selfish little bitches
She takes it upon herself
To spend fifteen more bucks

Tripping Balls

Not on snow cones
Oh no, not on Ice cream
This treat is called
GASOLINE!!
Open the garage door
Oh look
That red can
GASOLINE it says
Mothers, such decent human beings
Take hold of that rag
Do you hear it
Let the ear perceive
That Music
The sound of some child molester fun
Walk to the ice cream man
With his five dollars
Super special
Flavor of delight
That's right kids
Distract that son of a bitch
It's on the left
Open the hatch
The cap
Unscrew, unscrew, unscrew
The rag, shove it in
Douse it with gas
Leave your self a trail
Lil miss betty Crocker
Did you grab the matches?
OH NO!
Best run back
In such organization
Things are bound to get lost
Think, think, think
Where, oh where, did you place that book?

Gocni Schindler

Like a light bulb
The eyes race
Like shooting up with crack cocaine
Those pesky matches
Always outta arms reach
Keeping that little brat safe
Hurry, hurry, hurry
Don't want to be late
Out the door, down the driveway
Approach the ice cream man
He gives a toothers five-dollar smirk
Soccer mom of the day races through his mind
Loving it when silicone tits bounce
Wanting to give this Soccer MILF a special Creamy treat
Directly from his love gun
Views you in your sluttiness
Just another dog, just a piece of meat
His mind already undressed Mommy
She's always so alone
Home, with only a dildo
Light that match
Grab little Timmy by the arm,
The snow cone hits the ground
RUN, RUN, RUN
Murder is FUN!
Scream
"Oh, Ice Cream man!"
SCREAM!!!
As those who know show their tits
Eyes; explode across the globe
Mr. Fire finds its home
Explosions; Oh, glorious EXPLOSIONS
Little chunks of colored ice
Fall back to earth

Tripping Balls

For the ice cream man
Is floating away with his harp
Devils claw for what belongs to them
The Pervert isn't going anywhere
They know what he's done
They helped him along
Like good friends
Ice cream man falls
Like a deflated balloon
Nowhere to run
To hell with you
For being corrupt
Its five fucking bucks
Three times a day
FIVE dollars with tits
Oh, house wife, oh, mother of three
Oh, protector of that throne
Who spreads her legs wide for the master to see!
White pickets with stains of red
From a terrible ACCIDENT!
Is that what you said?
Give us a faint
Pass on out
Another miraculous tear
Oh dear,
It's an actress's day
Lose consciousness
Perfection from the drama stage
You deserve an award
Give you a damn Oscar
Or some golden globe
Don't worry, Mommy dearest
Two eyes
Stuck in some sockets
A horny old bastard

Looks at your tits
While he sits upon a white throne
OLD MAN JIZ
Thy mind, gone
Bye, bye, memory
Another dead visitor
To play imagination with
Dementia after all
Know not where you belong
Where you came from
Give heed to nothing
Take care of no one
Says the old soul.
Looking through glass
The soul
Old, worn out
Eyes that work
Looking at Mommy tits
Dick hard in the hand
Stroking what is left
Medication reacting fast
No more pleasure stack
Those eyes seen that
Seen while squeezing one off
An old man smoking a cigarette
In some pile, O aids wreck
In that
"AUTOMOBILE!"
Waves, as two stumps, once called legs
Whip across the road
Murder in the first degree
The old man waves back
Too old to care
Just doesn't give a damn
Left to rot by those he loved

Tripping Balls

Rest of his days
Disease infests
Relatives just wait
Money in the BANK
It's what they expect
Rewards you know
Rewards, for watching someone pass away
One thing left
One thing to look forward to
THREE TIMES A DAY
Hoping to cum
Milf tits, Soccer moms
He watches them all
As they bounce
To the Ice cream truck
Those middle-class silicone tits
The old man begs
"Please dick, don't fail me now!"
Yes, little Timmy, yes, yes, yes
Please drop that ice cream cone
His tongue licks the window
Only something is a miss
This day was something new
Milf tits is starting a fire
What is she doing?
That was a big explosion
The concussion explodes the window
Knocking him to the floor
Brings old man back to the war
The CNA walks in
Old man with his dick in his hand
Then it's, oh well
Pop another pill
Let that sun cum down
Grab the young CNA upon her ass cheek

Gocni Schindler

Horney old devil
You can still get it up
Watch, your old world cum undone
Its madness in the pants
To be horney has a price
She gives you a shot
Your mind goes numb,
Think not ol'timer
Your life is done
Last breath, Heart attack
They'll toss you in a box
Everyone happy now
The Poodle Society, Big donation
Didn't see that one
Fucking cockroach family
HENRIETTA POOR FAT BITCH
Months pass
Three convicts cleaning a ditch
Remains found
Bones, not from dog
Sure, wasn't a Lucy the ape girl
Hell no
Not from a squirrel
It wasn't no Sasquatch
Its HENRIETTA
Poor, Poor, Henrietta
Husband, not so ball less now
In the back of a squad car
Sitting next to Milf Tits
Holding onto the remains
of an ICE CREAM SANDWICH.
Just smiles
All of them, all smiles
All day long
Ask me questions

Fucking apes could solve crimes faster
Thanks for using a computer
They got questions
Ask away
It's called
BEST FRIEND
It's called
ATTORNEY
Rights you know
Give me council
Pay for it all
Nothing you can do
Lawman, it's all just speculation
The soul is already gone
The system
Our grim reaper
Possess these things
Makes a profit
Selling death
HENRIETTA shouldn't have been such a bitch.
The End

Better Writer

Pretty little flowers, heart's content
write me something.
I want my love back
Please, please, Please
I want to experience special
I want to FEEL once again!
Make me loved, cherished
Make me, adored
Give it to me, unique
Amazingly hot
Inside the melting pot
The crotch, get it wet
The orgasm spreads
With Passions, tingling in my being
Attach a pretty picture, meaningful AMBIENCE
Read me the text
Stolen from an ancient man
My hallowed, now fulfilled
My mouth, full of bile from your instant success
It spews onto the ground
Write in the small pond
Viable Proof, over these used shoes
Write, oh, writer, write
The world, a beautiful place
Toss it some glitter
Glue stick the bitch with beautiful surroundings
What on earth did you experience?
It was just stolen from an old man's book
Another person's life of hardships
Give us those moments
Fleeting times to paper
Uplift me with something spiritual
Bring me home

Tripping Balls

Let me caress your throne
To guide me in what you believe is right
Imagine all those pretty little things
Bitch, you couldn't write to save your soul
All that you spew is falsity
Suckers take hold from not understanding
They all walk alone
In it for the profits, fame, nothing more
The following to give you nicer things than most
Pretending to help people
Just another leach to bleed them dead
Guiding those to a promised land
Follow the writer, who proclaims, you too can have it all
Under the guise of 'Do what though wilt, though'.
In the name of selfishness
The mob of people you have robbed
Should come for your neck
Write, oh, writer, WRITE!
Give it to us beautiful
Lie to us all
You deserve a paycheck after all.

Mental Blues

1994 BCMW......
Another time of horror
Sitting at a table
With four mental cases
No worse off than I
Medicated, so fun, it's a game
Time to make the brain numb
Cocks all shriveled
Just limp
Entertainment with a mummified dick
Just sitting there drooling
It used to be a hell of a wingding
With Crack Cocaine
With fancy, cheerful drugs
Escape the reality of life's hell
Damn door, it doesn't really exist, does it?
Bang head against it
Revolving constantly, just spinning free
Don't you know Doc, it makes the world turn
The crazy cunt with her hands in her pants
Babbling on as she stares out the window
"Not in a box, nor with a fox
No not on a train, nor in the rain
It's all in this brain!"
Just shut the fuck up, I scream
The brain pain doesn't go away
Give me more drugs
To me, give it, please
Mind, oh mind, not mindless
Extortionist, unlawful, feeble
Everyone is fucking insane
Let's go nuts, tear this cage
Just pure resolute

Tripping Balls

Needing everybody's NOTHING
Rip these clothes away
Run the streets naked, the way it's supposed to be
Let the ding-a-ling feel the earth's breeze
The orderly doesn't like us naked
The talk lands me in the white button room
Nothing to obtain, just mindless leading mindful
The bearded man, he's intelligent
on the daily, my personal mind fuck
Sucking that pipe like a cock
His breath smells like shit mixed with mint
Disparaged imposter
Another Freud in the system
Another fuck the people Bernays
Softly he approaches
Like a fictional friend
Always asking, interrogating, deciphering
He just wants it all
Just another experimental rat
More notes on my symptoms
This mind to write a book about
I'll make the bastard a million-dollars
Stealing these dreams
Tearing away the thoughts
In my mind, He's playing
"DIG DUG!"
Smoke comes out of his nostrils
See the evil, indeed
Please sir, please master
Oh please, don't put me-
Shit!
Not in the waste can
The Devil is in there
Oh, god no, please, please not again
Not in the waste can

Alive for nothing but time
Physically trifle
Physically thinking
Mentally spiritually nothing
Societally broken
Only thing to do
Take the medication
Follow the rules
Issues some pharmaceuticals
Eyes perceive, weakness None
Need to play along, to get away from insanity
Spit them out, spit them into thy feeding hand
Fat bitch orderly, surely, she doesn't like that
No sir, not one bit!
Understanding in unknowing
Fucking my brain, my mind numb
This soul is all but drained
Wait a damn minute
Feels like I'm floating
I'm flying, like a bird
Let's flap these arms, no one to catch me
Start to finish, same results
Seeing the real, isn't seen in the real
Pushing, push, moving, move
Move to pushing
Push to moving
No mind to mind
Caring, the spirit again
White dicks in a black hole
Equal in size, constant the war
Never ceasing, no to a victor
Definitely a loser
Just a constant standstill
Tickets to ride
In the mind

Tripping Balls

On the short bus
Shovel another pill
Open the hatch
It's down for fun
Forced the water
Whiteness equals darkness
Plus, one in the hole
Three, just a never-ending disease
An ageless futility
Warring for the better seat
The better
Warring for something
Not worth the war
Both insignificant
both, just vile, just ash
I'd say shit
Though, they'd like that
Mind-set, fucking corrupt
Came from nakedness
From nothing
Happily, will take it back
It's always, always
In the manner, you have come
Repayment for the lease
Signed, the moment those lungs breathed
Doors locked, feeble weakness
Tries to re-open
No way out
Like a mouse trapped
Suffocate, suffocate, rodent scum
SUFFOCATE......
Take a last breath
The lost
Stand still
Like blinded deer

Told to sit, sit back down
Get on the ground
Commanded by the fat bitch nurse
With a pack of wolves, called orderly white shirts
Asinine, just pissed yourself
Worse than dogs
Get in, fool
Master locks the cage
Shovel in the shit
BIG PHARMA
They got billion-dollar cures
Liked being labeled
Same as food
Open, chew, swallow
open, chew, now fucking swallow human parasite
REPEAT
Swallow, puke
See it all come out, draw a pretty picture
Making art, from the bile with your tongue
The new play thing while locked away
Locked, straight jacket, restrained
Bang your head, its padded, need to keep safe
The test subject to bring clarity for the book deal
Dummy, you're clinically insane!
Never to see the outside
The eyes
Dimming, as the spirit looks out
Miniature port holes
Its mace in the face if you get in the way
Freedom actions away
Freedom chuckles from being shamed
The window just easily kicked out
FEAR! Keeps us inside
Lost donkeys on the waffle express
Fighting each other

Tripping Balls

Over personal nothingness
Worthless minds, stuck in a box
Suffocating, puffed up on the outside
Puffed like a flaming marshmallow
That will save them as they sit down
Doing what they're told
Dogs get better rewards!
Society is better off
Here comes the needle
Time for your dose
Hoping for a lethal injection
Give some electricity to the brain
We need a guillotine
Take away the insane
For the best, save the rest
Insane practice
Morals are without ethics
Down the toilet
FLUSH, FLUSH, FLUSH
Just another revolving door
Its spins, spins, spins
It's out the window
Or one simply doesn't live
They all scream the same
 "Die with the system!"
Oh, God help me
It's all over
God doesn't care, mortal, this place houses no god
No reward, boundless yet gagged
Burnt in the box
Strap'em down
Electrode to the temple
It's just a little
SHOCK
Never learns

Do what's been done before
All that is known
Caress the Devil's nut sack
Weep within yourself
God is on vacation, man
Who really is the monster?
Glad you asked
Both are trapped in a box
One has the power
The other has none
That's not James
that's Patient X #627637647
It's OK
Kill'em with the term
Psychiatric science
Each day, society creates
A new monster.
Then ponders, what created the monster?
To fulfill the need
 Acting the part
Mentally confused

HOBO'S LOST PARADE

Sober mental state
Wave farewells
Soon will be off
Wind takes hold
Sailing away on a ship named IMAGINARY
Onto the horizon
Off, to the high scene
Over to rainbows
Play with unicorns, magical things
Whimsical big, BIG, dreams
Dreaming sheep, dream
Amongst the wolves, of course
Grand Ideas
Nothing to expect
Pocket with a few cents
Mainly dirt, mainly lint
Cock in a cage
Fighting to win, yet down its kept
Branded with iron rods
Mankind cock-marked for the world
Naysayers, lay hold
Stoned near death
Pick it up, wipe off self
Let the past rest
Heal thy brokenness
Limping ends never quit
Hobbling lost down open roads
No deals
Angels who lost the way
Reality jet packs
Another white light
To a darkness state

Gocni Schindler

Seeking what is felt
Longing what should have been
Confused, lost souls
Hell, to help the world
Trying to impress
Heart not willing for wanting less
Materials equals emptiness
Another traveler's tale
Hobo's lost parade
Homeward bound
Welcome, grand old stage
Father waving weeping child's return
Solid embrace
Tears, melting ground like acid rain
Sorrows, found not on that day
Head downwardly hangs
Strong hand uplifts the chin
Many wrong turns
Answers not returned
Days upon days
Lost in an endless haze
Questions none resolved
Inner peace floating along
Wanting it all
Frail body worn out cold
Just writing it down
Worlds at thy feet
It's a universal law
Laws, outside of common sense
A hindrance to growth
Hobos lost parade

IN LIKES WITH LUCIFER

When I was a child, I was a bit odd.
My love thought I was in likes with a Lucifer!
I was sent to a priest.
Priest looked upon me with disgust
Disdain upon my burnt tortured state
He thus said:
"Recant vile sinner, RECANT!"
I looked upon the priest while he sprayed me with spit
White holiness rained cool over me.
My lips gave utterance to this
"TNACER, rennis eliv ouy tnaceR"
The Priest struck my face, held a crucifix against my head
told me to renounce a Lucifer as he read from the book
I looked upon the priest with compassion thus stating.
"I don't know a Reficul!"
"Why do you practice acts of hate?"
Rage engulfed the good minister, as I stated
 "As of now, you look like a reficul! Not a
servant of that fictional character dog you claim to follow."
The Priest became furious, ultimately, beating me with the baby doll's leg he grabbed from the crib in some miniature barn.
He had no idea I suffered from DYSLEXIA! He thought that some Lucifer was inside of me. This is the messenger for the highest.
The message, beat the child, beat the child, come on, all you ass kissers in the first and second pews, get your hands up and repeat after me
BEAT THE CHILD, BEAT THE CHILD, BEAT THE CHILD
THIS IS THE MESSENGER FROM THE HIGHEST

Gocni Schindler

THE MESSAGE.
BEAT the dyslexic CHILD.

Religion: Destroyer of the mind, hope for the grave

Oliver

Oliver was steadfast
Believer in Karma
Apparent in consciousness
Mommy loved unequally
Ambiguity for Salvation
Sleeping with anonymous
Universal in mannerisms
Closed minded avocations
Keeping with brutality
Slaying reliable, Oliver
Die, Oliver, die.
Sad, the fate of little Oliver
The news proclaimed
Life so full of hate
Some analyst wench
Pretending to care
Trying to play journalist
Sun bright smiles
Rodent, who doesn't give a shit
Oliver's unfortunate fate
Is all she states

The Great American Con Job

When they put war on something
It's real meaning
Time to screw the American people.
In the 80's,
It was cool to have a commercial frying eggs.
This is your brain, it said.
This is your brain on Drugs!
Any questions?
"Yes, I have questions!"
"Shut up, stupid!"
The response:
I still did drugs, it was fun
This shit box world requires them.
Mother earth knows best,
It's why the weed was given
Needing something to help cope with the mess.
The answer to the question is simple!
The war on drugs, another con job
Screwing the American people on lives, prosperity
Prison for addicts solves zero.
It benefited society not one bit
Having zero effectiveness
Illogically dumping billions
Into this wasted program!
Congratulate ourselves for being voiceless
For taking the government's
Enormous cock in our ass
Like a baby's nook, we sucked it dry
Living the great American con job
Just another war

When I was young the most beautiful woman in the world was Mom. The second, Cher, the Music Super star, who is utterly beautiful.

PARADISE

The Homeless man's eyes, searching the blue sky.
The streets of the city.
People, hustling by in the 99-degree heat. Walking down the sidewalk. A man, a woman, a child. A little lad, with a
red balloon! The Homeless man's eyes
connect to the young lad. A memory, from a former life.
The young lad tugs on his father's shirt.
"Papa, papa, why is that guy sitting on the curb?"
The man kneels, looks the child in the eyes then looks over to the homeless man who wreaks of stink from the street. Just smiles
"Sometimes, son, life can be very CRUEL."
Looking his son in the eyes, the man reaches into his pocket
pulling out some change. Placing the change in the young lad's hands
"Here, go give this to the man."
The boy, vex, yet courageous!
Walks over to the homeless man.
The young lad's shadow, casting over
The homeless man looking up.
Sweat profusely with dirt dripping off his brow. The lad's
eyes a spellbinding blue.
The lad, wanting to speak.
Fear, gripping his tongue!
Hand shaking. Lifting his arm, releases the coins. Homeless
Man's eyes are still locked to the young lad's.
Coins bouncing off the concrete.
Echoing, Homeless man's mind in a still frame. What

seems like eternity, his head, rotating downward. Eyes, watch
In amazement! Coins going to and fro!
Hands not moving. The lad, bolting back to the man, back to the woman, back to love. It's a mom and dad!
Homeless man's hands move, grabbing up the money.
Like a chicken, plucking its food, gathers up the
Coins while looking up. The boy with the red balloon, walking away. The boy's head turns slowly, his mesmerizing
blue eyes, looking back at the homeless man
The lad bumping into someone, lets loose the red balloon!
Homeless man watches its ascent!
The lad vanishes into the mass.
Eyes follow the balloon as his mind goes into a dream while a familiar voice echoes in his heart.
"Ronin, RONIN? Where are you Ronin?
I need your help in Troy's room."
Ronin's eyes glued to a computer screen. Glued to something
Deemed at the time, important. Yet he miraculously responds
"On my way, I'm finishing an email to my client!"
Ronin closes his laptop then heads through the foyer, runs
up the stairs into Troy's room. The outline of his wife, her
blond hair, her figure, races through his mind.
"Ronin, can you please hang this red balloon mobile up here over Troy's bed."
Ronin frowning. "Why on earth are we hanging a red balloon
mobile over his bed? Why not something cool, like jet fighters or spaceships?"

She doesn't even think about it
"Because, that is what Troy has picked out of the magazine."
Ronin climbs on the bed screwing the eye hook into the Ceiling, then, she hands him the red balloon mobile. He hangs
the mobile, as they watch the red life-like balloons spin. Suddenly the memory is broken to the sounds of a deep voice
"Scumbag trash, move on; you can't be here!"
The balloon vanishing into the sun, Ronin's head moves slow.
A slave to the system, enforcer of policy, jolly Ol'Police officer is trying to communicate
"Shit for brains, you deaf?"
The Officer getting annoyed relatively
quick kicks Ronin in the arm.
"I am not going to ask again, now move it!"
Ronin looking at the officer, gets on his knees, grasping the
ragged cup while gathering his tattered jacket, stands and
walks away.
Walking, Ronin gazes upward, trying to find the red balloon
in the sky, a sky so vast, so empty, yet with no avail. Walking down the street,
half dehydrated from the heat, cuts down an alley. A familiar
area. Taking the change out of his ragged cup, placing the
coins into his left pocket. The only pocket he has with no
holes. Lifting his cup up under an air conditioner. Catching the water that drips off.

Down the alley is the back of the Chinese restaurant.
Ronin filling the cup halfway drinks the warm water.
Walking down to the back of the Chinese restaurant looks
around. It's a crime to take food from a dumpster.
Lifts on the locked dumpster just enough to get his hand
to slide in. Pulling out a hand-full of day old noodles mixed
with a hardened white rice. He places the filth in his mouth
and begins to chew.
Gravity pulls a piece of rice off his lip. It slowly falls to
the ground as Ronin's mind fades away to the memory of a
different day. A day to be like no other day
"Hey, dad, is that my Chinese noodles?"
Ronin, walking through the door at the hospital room looks at
his Son!
"Yes, it is, had Chou's make it just the way you wanted
 with no vegetables, got you plenty of soy sauce!"
Sitting on the bed, Ronin pulls out the food. Troy trying to
sit up.
"Dad, that smells great!"
Ronin, looking up sees the green colored fluid flowing out of
the IV and into his son's arm. Smiles to hide a pain
"You're my brave little man!"
Just then, the phone rings!
Ronin reaches over and picks it up
"Hello."
It's a voice he knows well, though her tone is distressed!
"Ronin, I just got off the phone with the Doctor!"
She Pauses. Ronin picks up the pieces

Tripping Balls

"Honey, what is it?"
Ronin's wife slows to respond!
"Is Troy by you?"
Ronin grabbing the phone walks over to the window looking
at Troy trying to eat the food
"Not exactly, why?"
She lets out a sigh!
"We have a meeting with the Doctor, I'm heading over to
his office now from work!"
Ronin, looking at Troy now has an emptiness in his voice
"What's going on?"
She can barely muster the words somehow though they protrude!
"Ronin, the blood results came back, they are not good!"
She pauses to hold back the tears that don't stop
"The Doctor will explain everything to us, this stuff still confuses me, can you meet me there, please?"
Ronin looking out the window in disbelief
"I'm heading there now, babe.... I love you!"
She doesn't respond, how can she
Though, she is wishing that Ronin for once would tell her
that everything will be OK.
Ronin listening the phone goes dead, hanging up the phone,
looks over to Troy
"Hey kiddo, your mom and I have to go see Doctor."
Leaning over he kisses his son's bald head.
"I love you."
Troy looks up to his dad with a smile on his face
"I love you too!"
Ronin begins to leave; Troy calls out to his father

"Dad?"
Ronin turns and looks at Troy
"Yes."
Troy looks at his dad with a strong face
"Everything will be OK, don't be afraid, dad,
I'm tired, my chest hurts; I'm going to rest."
Ronin smiles at Troy, then turns and walks out of the room.
Heading over to the elevator. His mind Flashes!
Thoughts race through his mind of the birth of his son.
His curly blond hair, those beautiful blue eyes'. Another elevator ride ten floors down, seems like an eternal descent
One that's been done a thousand times already,
only this time it's different.
The mind focuses on Troy's first steps, his
first tooth.
All the things taken for granted come flushing in.
Exiting the elevator, his mind just places one-foot forward
 heading over to meet with his wife
The office has a pale blue paint scheme with pictures of all
the children that suffered from cancer! A wall size bulletin
board of the ones who lived, as well as the ones who died!
A memorial, of the courageous little warriors.
A squeaky voice from behind a piece of glass
"Good afternoon, Ronin."
Ronin looks and a wide-eyed nurse whom he knows on a first
name basis is staring at him in the doorway. A nurse, he met,
three years prior.

"Oh, hello, the wife and I have an appointment with the Doctor."
The Nurse looking at Ronin.
"Yes, I know. Just have a seat, he'll be with you shortly."
Ronin turns to sit as a voice echoes in
"Ronin?"
Turning he looks to see his wife walking through the door
They greet each other with a long-standing hug, almost like
Strangers that just met.
"Don't worry!"
Is uttered out of Ronin's mouth. Tears pouring out of his wife's eyes, like a flood. Her nails digging into skin
"I can't not worry, I can't!
As Ronin and his wife are talking. The good Doctor walks
through the doorway.
"Oh, hi guys, please, come down to my office!"
The Doctor looking at the Nurse
"Would you call the Psychologist down here please."
The Nurse looking at Ronin and his wife with a disheartened
frown for she knows what this call really means
"Yes Doctor."
They all sit down in the office awaiting the arrival of Psychologist. Small talk is heard from Doctors office. For no
one really wants to ask a question that is already known.
The Psychologist walks in with her cup of coffee.
"Hi everyone. I would say hi to you Doctor; but we just
Conversed with each other 40 minutes ago,"
Doctor smirks at the Psychologist
"Psychologist, if you would have a seat, I'll begin."
The Doctor pulling out a binder the size of a law book

"There is no easy way to say this."
Ronin reaches and grabs his wife's hand. Grasping, a death
grip. She looks at Ronin, her eye's usually a brilliant blue.
Now, covered in a haze of red with a sea of glass from all
the tears she has shed. Ronin's eyes start to swell together
they look at the good Doctor.
"The blood results show that the cancer has spread, in the
three years of treatment the cancer started to remit
though the chemo is no longer working. It has spread
through the body at a much faster rate than anticipated."
Ronin, mustering the strength
"How much time do we have, Doctor?"
Doctor pauses a moment
"A few days or weeks, maybe a couple of months, at most."
The Psychologist interjects
"I would like to meet with you guys to help you cope with
this. Also, I have a group that gets together every
Wednesday, can I set that up for you?"
Ronin's Wife responds through a tear soaked voice
"Yes, please do."
Psychologist with a heartfelt voice.
"OK, I will dear! If you need anything, please call,
Anytime, I'll make myself available!"
Ronin and his wife leave the office. It's like ice all over
them. They say nothing, what can they say? The ride in the
elevator like they don't exist. No words, no comfort, just a

empty numbness. Ding, ding, ding, the doors open. Ronin
staring into the empty hall. His wife, exits the elevator.
Ronin like a baby, putting one foot in front of the other, starts to walk. A walk that they did a thousand times before.
The ceiling tiles are painted with art work from all the children from the tenth floor.
Walking down the hall they see emergency doors open. Bursting forth is a medical team.
Whom they know by name. Neither
Ronin nor his wife had any utterance left to speak. They turned the corner and were gone. Wife, frantically starts running, as if an intuition came over her. Ronin still in a comatose state, walking. Only to be awakened by the blood
curling screams from his wife.
Ronin, running, rounding the corner. Medical personnel in
and around Troy's room. Ronin gets to the door way peering
in. Troy's on the floor with blood pouring out of his mouth
and nurses pulling his wife away from their son.
She's in a rage of tears, screaming, kicking.
Trying to hold onto her only child
The medical team he knew by name, was trying to jump start
Troy's heart! Ronin, the room spinning, the lifeless body of
his son on the ground. The Doctor calls the time. The words
echo in slow motion in Ronin's ears. Ronin hit's the ground.

He surely didn't know that would have been the last time he
would've seen his son alive. Just note those words Ronin
"Everything will be OK Dad, don't be afraid!"
Screams, screams, screams are heard.
A foreign tongue.
Ronin, vision, coming around, laying on the ground, looking
up, through blur tear filled eyes. Reality sets in as he sees
a little oriental man shouting
"You, get out! Go, get!"
Ronin, grabbing hold of the dumpster, pulls himself up.
Ignoring the rambling from a language not his own,
Pushing past the screaming little oriental man.
Tears, pouring out of Ronin's eyes. The numbness runs wild in
his veins. The endless rage. The heart filled with
anger, pumping utter despair. Stumbles to the ground! His
face looks up to the sky. Tears, fall from his cheek like a
gentle rain as he screams the screams, to release the agony
Ronin's head falls to the ground. His hands dig and scrape
Ronin slowly picks himself up walking painfully
down the alley way. Blood drips from his fingers.
Pain nullified from the overwhelming sadness that always
remains. Walking into the sunset, his outline slowly dissipates

Tripping Balls

WHEN YOU LIVE ON THE STREET, REALITY IS A COLD, HARD, GROUND!
HARDENED HEARTS FROM THOSE AROUND...WELCOME, TO A MORAL SOCIETY IN THE BUSINESS AMERICA WE CALL PROUD

TIME IS NOT OUR FRIEND

Million times have I searched
For time, that came then went
Today, I only reflect
Countless thoughts bring me back
It was sheer seconds
Ones, I never wanted to end
In my hands, did you rest
Let me smell thy new scent
Snuggle you, bringing warmth to cold flesh
Till blue, a cruelty of death
Thy joy removed
Swells from wetted eyes
Rivers of pain, washed away
Nothing, what is left
Mercy, never to be felt
With an orange in his hand
A devil simply laughs
Million times have I searched
Upon a night time sky
Seeking a face never to be seen again
Time that came, then went
To hold you once again
Remember what was
Lost with time itself
Now aimlessly
Wondering down broken roads
Leaving pieces of myself
Other souls warming touch
Trying to find light
Darkness, that hideous friend
Knowing, no way back
Altered on this broken path
Just another shipwreck

Tripping Balls

No words nor hearts to mend
Lost, can never come back, in matters of flesh
A goodbye is never enough
For time is not our friend
Demise, our sure bet

Bad Management

From the shop window, the Manager peers out
His pride upon the floor
Watching all his little human Money Slaves hustle about
Doing their tasks, their jobs.
The Manager looks at his hand.
A hand, that in a former life, a former existence, would have
held some mighty whip.
The Manager yearns, more like wishes in a fantasy, to use a
whip on these slacker human money slaves. Parasites in his
mind, that just fill his company floor.
The Manager, looking at the ceiling, closes his eyes and takes a deep breath.
The air fills his lungs, like a sink fills with water.
Slowly he lowers his head, his eyes flash open in a psychotic fashion as he exhales.
The Manager turns on his heel like a well-trained Nazi SS
officer. Eloquently walking over to his phone.
Extends his arm, then retracts it, then extends it again.
Methodically, his thumb, index,
middle and ring fingers grasp the receiver.
While his pinky pushes the intercom.
Placing the receiver up to his ear, his mouth
speaking in an ultimate tone it's been well practiced.
No "um" in his vocal cords.
"Bob Smith, to the Managers office!"
The Manager slams the phone down then pushes play on his
CD player. Music blares through the speakers.
The Manager triumphantly returning to the window

Tripping Balls

his arm raises, looking at his Rolex that the company gave
him. The clock tic tocs away!
A fat balding man, wearing cheap fat
man slacks, hustles through the plant.
Bob Smith, sweating profusely, running hard!
The Manager, watching, with anticipation.
As Bob Smith is running.
A young geeky kid, with his hat on backwards,
wearing safety glasses. Operating a motorized pallet jack,
moving a pallet of parts.
Seeing all, like a god from the heavens, The Manager
eyes beholding his watch, sees all.
Marking the time, then lets his hands
rest on the window glass.
As he agitatedly awaits.
A Secretary walks into the office.
"Sir?"
The Manager does not speak, he doesn't need to, just raises
his hand to silence her! He doesn't want to listen, nothing is
more important, he is watching his fat supervisor run.
The Secretary rolls her eyes, then exits the
office.
Bob Smith moving fast, hustles his fat ass hard
Towards the Manager's office.
The Manager looks closer.
The young man moves the motorized
pallet jacket into the alley way.
The Manager with sheer excitement seeing all shouts out!
"KABOOM, CRASH, SMASH, YES that is what I like to see!"

Bob Smith crashes into the pallet of parts sending him head
over heels.
The Manager puts his hands in the air as if his
favorite team just scored some important point in a game.
Bob Smith's fat body bounces off the ground like a rubber
ball, he skids across the epoxy painted shop floor that's clean enough to eat off.
The young man in a state of shock puts
His hands on his mouth
Attempting to stop the instant laughter.
Bob Smith quickly gets off the floor, limping his way towards
The Managers office. An entire shop floor is in laughter.
The Manager, just shakes his head, peers at his watch, then frowns.
Bob Smith limping, attempts to hustle through a door, down
a hall then up a flight of stairs.
Blowing through another office door that states,
Managers Office. The dark-haired secretary just shakes her
Head. The Manager is looking out the window as an out of
breath Bob Smith enters
The Manager turns his head slowly, looking at Bob in utter
disgust.
Bob Smith, in his fat man shirt that is slightly
torn, slightly tattered. Sweat drips off his brow,
attempting to talk as he composes himself.
"You needed me... Sir Manager?"

Tripping Balls

The Manager looks at his watch, then his eyes lock with Bob
Smiths as he shakes his head.
The Manager walks to his desk, tapping the pause button on
his CD Player. Then meticulously addresses Bob.
"Bob, you know what I see on the floor?"
Bob Smith looks at the Manager with uncertainty.
"People working hard, Sir Manager."
The Manager takes a drink of his coffee.
Bobs Smith's mouth dry from running.
He is wanting with thirst.
"Lack of 100 percent productivity Bob, that's what I see!"
The Manager takes another drink,
he savors the liquid knowing
Bob is in need for he thirsts.
The Manager laughs then sets the coffee on his desk.
"MMMMMM, MMMMMM, MMMMM! That is some damn
good coffee!"
The Manager, looking at Bob.
"You ever have this Brand X?"
Bob anticipating that the Manager is going to give him a cup!
"No I haven't, it smells delicious though!"
The Manager grimaces a bit.
"Great, you should go to Blue Deli when you are not working, treat yourself to some of this, it's absolutely delicious. Maybe, also have one of them donuts, god only
knows you're never going to lose that belly, lard ass."
Bob starts to talk but the Manager over powers him!
"It took you over five minutes to get up here, do you think that is acceptable?"

Bob Smith looks at the Manager confused.
"Sir Manager, I think that I got up here in a proper amount of time."
The Manager looks at Bob in disgust.
"Bob you're thinking again, we had a talk about this once, do we need to have a talk again?"
Bob shakes his head for no
The Manager cracks a smirk
"No, is exactly right! The correct response is, you are sorry you weren't instantly here the moment I called for you! Gosh, look at you, you're sweating like a stuffed pig in an oven, just looking at you makes me want to shower."
The Manager sniffing the air as he walks near Bob.
"What is that, do you smell that, that god awful smell?"
Bob sniffing the air
"I don't smell anything."
The Manager sniffs around Bob
"It's you, what is that you're wearing?"
Bob nervously shakes his head
"I have a cologne on that my wife bought for Christmas, is that what you're smelling?"
The Manager sniffs again
"Bob, you smell like shit, don't ever wear that garbage to work again or I'll fire you."
The Manager walks towards the window
peering out at the disaster.
"I'm losing 15 percent of productivity Bob! 15 PERCENT!! Do
you have any idea, any possible knowledge on how that reflects on my bonus?"
Bob shakes his head for no
"It's probably not good, sir Manager!"
The Manager looks at Bob
"Not good is right! Do you know why it's not good?"

Bob scratches his head
"Your Managers don't seem to like it?"
The Manager shakes his head in disgust.
"No, tubby, my numbers are still good because I am above
80% effective, it's not good because my bonus pays out double at 95% effective. If I don't hit 95% effective, then my fucking Princess of a wife doesn't get her trip to the Bahamas. Not good, Bob, as I'll be forced to listen
to her stupid ass bitch all year long! Also, not good because this year, I want to buy myself a new corvette. Guess who is starting to cost me this desire, this WANT, this.... NEED?"
Bob fixes his shirt.
"The employees not hitting their targeted numbers?"
The Manager peers at Bob with hard intent.
"No, NO! You are, dumb shit!!
Because your leadership sucks a soft
cock, you are a damn prom queen when I need a tiger roaming free, wanting to KILL, to EAT! You don't seem to
have what it takes to really motivate, to really bust these cock sucker's balls down there, getting them to work. Hell, I mean look at that dumb fuck running the pallet jack, for an hour, for a fucking hour he has been doing the same fucking thing. Why is he even here? One Hour, Bob, he's costing me a percentage! He should be fired!"
The Manager walks up to Bob, eyeballing his shirt, then starts
to fix his collar.
"Look at you, a fat, worn out slob that stinks, with- wait! Is this
some egg from breakfast?"

Bob looks down at his shirt. The Manager flicks Bob in the
face for looking down.
"See, you don't even know if you spilled egg on yourself or not, fucking pathetic."
Bob Smith looks down.
"I'm trying, sir Manager."
The Manager looks at Bob
then walks back over to the window
examining the shop floor.
"Trying, trying, here is trying! I have a wife that tries
to be a worthwhile investment of some part of importance.
Yet, without action, is just as useless now as she was the first day that I met her."
Bob Smith looks at the Manager in awe and shock.
"But....why did you marry her then?"
The Manager with a grin, looks at Bob intently.
"I'm glad you asked Bob, the only value a woman has is a pussy!
Something I happen to like. I have a great talent to
find what I need in useless people like yourself.
Her mom looked good at an older age
so, I figured, she would too and she does!
She is in the gym every day and I wouldn't have it
any other way! Don't want to be married to some lard ass
after all, god, could you imagine
the financial hit I would take if
I had to divorce someone like that!"
The Manager looks at Bob
"You know what I mean?"
Bob frowns, The Manager cracks a half smile.
"Of course, you don't! You see, you're about that damn
useless too, it's just too bad you don't have a pussy

Tripping Balls

Bob, then perhaps, just maybe I could get something satisfactory from you. In fact, the only reason you're even still a supervisor is because you want to be me. I respect that! If everyone was me
the world would be a much richer place."
Bob looks at the ground. The Manager looks out the window.
"Bob, I want you to go down to that shop floor. I want your fat, gelatinous ass to crack a whip! I want the fear of me in these people. I want them to wet themselves when I walk down there. I want their heads to
hang low! I want my 95 PERCENTILE and I want it yesterday!"
Bob looks at the Manager with some fictitious smile. The
Manager looks at Bob squarely.
"What is so funny, did I tell you to smile?"
Bob quickly ditches the smile.
"No sir, Manger!"
The Manager looks out the window!
"Great, now fire that fucking freak idiot running the pallet jack wasting my percentage. The next time you're summoned to my office, I want you here in three minutes,
not five. Now, get the hell out of my site you repulsive pile of lard."
Bob stands there numb from the mental abuse
The Manager shouts out.
"MOVE IT, LARD ASS!"
Bob Smith takes off running while the Manager walks to the
window to see the new form of motivation that will be expressed across the shop floor.
The Manager examines his greatness, how his personal

motivation can move a fat mountain
as he watches an enraged
Bob Smith that is now releasing an onslaught of shouts and
screams across the shop floor. A young man, just one of the
money slaves with his hat on backwards wearing some geeky
safety glasses in a turquoise shirt has just been fired.
The human Money Slaves move faster as Supervisor Bob
tries to get every sweaty inch of work out of them that the
Manager has ordered. Its money over human life!
It's a corvette, make it a convertible!

Tripping Balls

VROOOM, VROOOM

THE MANDATE

Your EXISTENCE, is of ill repute! If you don't put the corporation first, putting the corporation foremost in your
existence. Then you will not succeed in this life.
Without the corporation, you are nothing!
We, at the corporation, bestow you the life that you so value.
When we find a way to eliminate you, we will!
The corporation will do so, without care, nor regret.
We have many puppets, many, to work cheaper than you.
It is about making profits.
Our products are of value to the consumer; which is also you!
Everything you do, is for the higher good of the corporation
You are not of value, you're just a means to an end.
The CEO, Board Members and stake holders are who matter
Thank you for being a citizen of the corporation
until we no longer need you!
If a worker has no Job, a worker has no money. Thus, a worker
cannot purchase a product. If no products are purchased, then the corporation will cease to exist.
What a beautiful concept this is.
Ship all jobs to a cheaper labor, calling it staying competitive,
Yet its priced as if Americans built it.
Then, sell it to Americans. Only soon, Americans won't have a
dollar to buy the shit product that is made with a cheap labor mind-set

Tripping Balls

Conscious mental thinking of common sense
From the new American Slaves in a foreign country
Making a product for people who live better
 So, what do I care if this product actually works?
Greed infested the land, America, already dead
Rich men, line their pockets, doing nothing to help their own

Gocni Schindler

As a child, I had no dad, he split to Texas. I was thankful I had Clint Eastwood and Mel Gibson to watch on the screen. It filled the void

B

Be the BusIness

IF ONE ONLY SEES THEMSELVES AS WHAT THE STANDARDS OF THE WORLD STATE THEY ARE, THEN THEY MINDLESSLY LOSE THE ABILITY TO KNOW THAT THEY ALSO WALK IN A HIGHER REALM. THAT THEY HAVE A GREAT PURPOSE ON THIS LAND. THE REALM NOT SEEN. WE ARE A SUPERNATURAL BEING, THAT CAN DO ANYTHING. TEACH SELF TO BE THIS BEING IN THIS LIFE AND THEY WILL ACHIEVE EVERYTHING WITH SWEAT

CHILD

Our Child is kicking a bee hive called the world
Our Child is poking it with sticks.
Not a good idea that we allowed Our Child to play outside
Most likely Our Child will get stung
Then we all will pay a dear price.
Time to Lock up Our Child!
Before the child destroys us all

For You

Never read into things that aren't
Under any condition, don't take for granted things that
are
Change the things that need to be changed
Fix what you can; remove what you can't
Take no one's words to heart that has no laudable wealth
Never let anyone stand in your way
Take hold of what you have for soon that will depart
As the sun and the moon fight for precedence
Always watch for your moment to make your mark
Copy no one else's life, be unique, be you
Hold true to what makes you happy
Dream like none before
Search the seas of madness to find what you need
Fight like no other, taking hold of what you want
As a majestic kite fly's free upon the mighty wind
Run fast with your decisions while remembering
The meek child's hand that guides the majestic beast
Yet mysteriously is still beheld by one tiny, feeble,
string
Cherish like no other, always remembering what you've
done
While knowing, what you'll never do again
Try this at least once
You may get burnt
I sure know I did
Though it's something one will never regret
LOVE full hearted, never hinder, it's unmeasurable in
wealth
With love, though, if the mercy of the sea is there
to give you another shot at what you've lost
take hold this time; don't let it go
Run baby, RUN!

Tripping Balls

Things that come twice
Will likely never come again
Release what hinders your life
Living like you're already dead
Yet living like you just popped out of the womb
In the moments of time we're but a glimpse
Do something extraordinary
Try it, who gives a shit
It's something, isn't it
Live with nothing, so you experience everything
Don't be naïve in life, nothing is easy
Treasure beauty; it's really inside
Never kill the spirit; nor wound a soul
Bloody wounds will mend in time
Though never a broken soul
Help those of lesser place
As if you're in the same boat
Seek not fame, nor fortune
Just an honest goal
In doing so, will receive what you're looking for
Take time to feel with your hands
touch with your toes
Listen intently
Remember the sweet
To give place for the sour
Never misguide a child
For that consequence, will be at your door
Failures are only a learning curve
Attempts are what counts
Let not the world shame you with discomfort
Take what you will to try again.
Evil monsters will come, they will go
Meet a group of assentator's along the way
Many soulless bastards that lost their stay
Think often about thy own road

Gocni Schindler

Look deep to find your core
Understand things aren't in your control
Try to be happy
YOU ARE WORTH MORE THAN YOU KNOW

Be the clown, not the cow

The human entity is more capable
Than what is taught
It is a bad programming
Mind fucked with television
With garbage, educated in schools
In fake church pews
Humans, not trained to look beyond the box
Not informed to actually think
Brainwashed to obey some higher form of societal rule
The man on the moon
A sad system of doom
Only one outcome!
Everything is a lie
Those who carry on with the lie
Simply those who dislike the truth
Did you learn to OBEY or did you learn to Think
Be the clown, not the cow

Machine

Traveling
To the tune
From a dull melody
A former life
Just melancholy
Men, white beards
Fucking frowns; always disdain
Faces of void stamped into the machine
Why do they despise
Cause such pain
Time, that frenemy, such villainy
Barter me real, barter me a slave
Take away this energy
Merge my soul to the machine
Cocoon me in bailer's twine
Blast this vessel into space
Marvel at thy unraveling
Take notice of this shape
Yield to my crossing
Give it a moment's stay
Capture my essence
Keep it in your grace
Tenderize my hard shell
Like a piece of meat
Hurt it, make it bleed
Wash away past pains
Merge your soul into me
Mend your life while mending mine
One being, the machine
Gather into a pool of water
Where the spirit of life resides
Taking notice by careful study

Tripping Balls

Close attention, verify the details
Where goes the machine
Mind as large as the bird
Flowing free, high upon the sky
Riding the wind waves
Traveling to the end free with bliss
The woman, who crushed a heart
Black haired witch
Deceit was her gift.
Woman, giving Judas kiss
Beast was loved
More than self, truest regret
Love never regrets love
Wretchedness my mask
A Face of void, stamped into the machine
I hope to see you upon the machine
Drenched in gear oil
Pounded by the shaft
A shameful mess
All for a machine

Wanted Invisible

The Invisible, not the wanted
In the world, I am but an invisible name
Words spoken, knowledge forebear
No ability to have, only fruitlessness
World holds no value for no self-esteem
Seeking what is never known
Life, pitiless in sight
Time is but a revolving door
Turning slowly with a sign stating
I've been here before
An honor, lost long ago, denied yet again
Emptiness, grips all human beings
This frail, mortal mind, lost it all
Brought to the whipping post
To be scorned with self-ruinous hate
Transgressions, never committed, except upon self
The invisible, never seen, nor heard
Words, uttered from the pure
Never taken into consideration
Downcast, forgotten, is what the invisible holds
The invisible beholding no purpose
Understand, they don't belong
Existing amongst the souls that walk
The invisible, always looking for a place
Path is barren, Pathway lost
Nothing is the crown that crests the head
Labels to titles, not given just personal shame
Loneliness is the robe worn
Tattered, torn, on consequence trail
Boots of inadequacy, worn thin
The kingdom empty
What remains, but things not seen
The invisible with a mind of silence

Like a dirty secret, filled with shame
Neither accepted, nor acknowledged
Never welcomed, always lost
Head cast down with personal shame
Lost is the invisible that takes no worth in self

Whimpering Complaint

Can't the gates just open
Everything, always a battle
Have to just watch as it slips
Through fingers worn thin
Like grains of sand
Floating down to the ground
Building a small wall
No arms to reach over the top
Wanting what can't be held
Having what wasn't wanted
Fighting, to obtain what seems impossible
Through fires, getting hot
Through blood, feeling, faint
Another time, paraded down some street
A returning conqueror, the champion
Bestowed upon a famous city
Some glory, that earned its mark
Faced in the dark, this life walked
Unending shadows that linger
Live ravenous wolves
Waiting for thy knee to fall
To feast on this body
Ripping, tearing
The heart still beats
While being the feast
Lamp's flame to subdue
Last energy evades
Off thy lips
Final breath escapes
Like a red mist, freezing in the air
Time to gather that red mist back
Like a vacuum sucking it in
The oxygen brings life back

Tripping Balls

Wrecked body, fuck that
The knee that fell will be raised again
That lamp light will return
In a vengeance stance
Burn shit to the ground
Vicious shadows
Those wild wolves on the prowl
Plummeting dead carcasses.
Nothing more, fictional work, dream world
What we want it to be
The gates don't open
Rip them down
Lay waste to the kingdom
World wants to battle
Then with the ripening of the fruit
Fight long, fight hard
Fight until the end brings it down
Don't ever quit, never give in
Allow yourself to stand
Be not what will keep yourself down
Not ever is it allowed

Fully Cooked

The disaster
A tray of meatloaf
Only thing she can cook
This Man is pissed
Meatloaf under cooked
Hand wields a hatchet
Swing away, this wench needs to pay
Another travesty
A murdered rose bush
The very next day
Societal cunt's line up
Never have they
Who could do such a thing
Murder a poor defenseless rose bush
Empathy is abounding
When vagina is around
Another fake soccer mom
Seeing what a lonely house wife does
Justified by the law of self
Shaking her ass for not the man that paid
No, the many that pay
Cost of admission, attention
Behind the scenes
The text sets the stage for a back-door date
Anticipation makes the play
The rich man's trophy display
She spends the money
Helps take the pain away
It's another Yoga class,
Just a whore in a spandex
Another flirtatious squirt
filling the void
Just as long as the meatloaf

Tripping Balls

Is fully cooked!

Meet Sara and Dave

They have two children
It's the American dream
White picket fences
That imaginary tale
Hollywood fills our heads.
Work full time to pay the bills
Sara also works nights
At the local restaurant
Gotta make ends meet
Dave tucks the kids in bed
While they ask where mommy is
Sara and Dave get up at 5 AM
They get ready to go slave
In a system corrupted with pulped wood
Their kids raised in the care system
Might as well be locked in a cage
Sara and Dave slave away
For some bullshit
That society says they need
It's too bad
Sara and Dave didn't stop to ask themselves
Is this how things really should be
Though, poverty, the alternative
Cause you can't live in a system
This fucking corrupt
Without working your hands
Without working your mind
Into oblivion in order to survive
America sure is great isn't it
Sara and Dave

Tripping Balls

**It's easy to survive
when you're in the Government**

patience for the laugh

Sitting here,
At this magazine stand on the BLVD
Waiting my damn turn
For cigarettes, of course
Some old woman, left in the world alone
Ahead of me
Can't make her mind up
The rude ass Persian working the stand
If he disrespects her again
It's going down
Sick of these clowns thinking they own it all
Well, they kind of do, but still
Fuck you with getting old
Losing your damn mind
Pissing in your pants all the time
No need to be rude
The asshole behind me
Keeps pushing
As if it's going to magically
Make me disappear.
Turning my head
"Is there a problem here?"
His deep black eyes don't back down
Just nods for no as he pushes again
"What, do you have to piss or something?"
Some Non-American gibberish spews from his mouth
Fucking Mexi-Something or other
But this guy must go
The old woman left alone in the world
Paying with coins from her purse.
Fuck this, I tossed the greedy Persian a ten
The old woman, left in the world alone
Tries to say no, I understand, it's a pride thing

Tripping Balls

I just insist that I need to buy some smokes
Have a nice evening
She says thank you and leaves
My turn finally
The Persian asks what I need.
I tell him nicely, one 8 ball, 3 White Lightning's
and 2 packs of smokes.
Make them Marlboro Lights, because suddenly
I'm worried about dying and need the lighter smoke
Stupidly, the Persian is looking for
The first two requests,
As if he would have them or some shit
Dude behind me pushes again.
The Persian tells me he can't find an 8 Ball
and White something or others
Who the hell can tell what he said
The asshole doesn't speak English very well
No one speaks English anymore in Hollywood
Don't worry though
I'll gladly press 4 or 5 for English
It's the very least I can do
Not like we live in America, that country is dead news
Pushed again, mother fuckers my attitude
This asshole behind me
Just give me the smokes then
He grabs the smokes
That's twenty.
I'm fucking confused
Twenty for what?
The two packs of smokes
My Phone starts to sound off
Jesus the virgin birth, what is this
I toss the Persian twenty and grab the smokes
Flinging from my mouth
Keep the change, Ya filthy Persian animal

Answering my phone, it's my actor friend
Fuck, you don't need to know
I don't want to give the prick a larger ego
Not to mention
I'd probably have to pay him
It's a trademarked name after all.
Actor clowns, the whole lot
Hey Bro!
Yes, how can I help you
I hate to drop this on you need some help
Don't we all
Shit guy, this is serious, you around town?
No man I'm nowhere to be found
Serious have a huge issue
Seems it's always an issue over flow the washer again
Really come'on need your help bad like yesterday bad
Oh, the luxury, dare I ask
Guy Someone stole my identity is using it on some bull shit dating website asking people out thinking it's me this is some serious shit PR agent said Facebook Fan page blowing the hell up wanting to know if I'm available. Manager getting calls, fuck the tabloids you have to help!
STOP!
There my dear readers this is where we Stop the bus of insanity. Take a deep breath and laugh. I couldn't help but laugh, laughing my ass off. I don't think he appreciated the gesture. Wasn't sure with all my laughing. I think he told me off a few times. Composing myself yet again let us continue
So, what can I do?
You know, you're the computer guru, fix it or something.
I can't fix that, email the dating site, tell them it's not you!

Tripping Balls

That's it you can't help me!
Not with that
Click, the phone goes dead
I laugh again as I pack my smokes
God the irony of it all
Open the goodness and light up
Great is the reward of a cigarette
You can't pay for that type of entertainment
Blessed is he who has
The Virtue of patience

Little Being

In the time of the Giants walked a little Being
The little Being was always trying
Thinking about what he wanted to do
Chasing paper airplanes
Whilst running after dreams
Dreams, of kitty toad poles floating in the air
Time places the dust, that the air removes
Yet, time places the dust once again
Giants, attempting to discover new ideas
While the old idea is never used
The laughter of children
Echoing through the halls of crowded spaces
Unused toys that fill market square
Made from the furnace in a place called China-world
Products that flutter throughout the house
Giving kids
Scraps of paper, of cardboard
Putting together with a heart of fantasy
Waste fills to the sky
Endless need for more
Just continues to grow
The Being
looking around
Wondering
"What will become of this?"
The Giants float around
Paying no attention
To the destruction being done
The Being holding a coin that states
"MOMMA SAID MONEY MADE THE WORLD GO AROUND!"
The Being met with other little Beings that asked

Tripping Balls

"What's the word?"
The world
"WORD IS!"
A world of the Giants
Gone recklessly scarce.
The little Beings scream with madness
Giants annoyed at their disturbance give them food
"THIS WILL SHUT THEM UP!"
No one wants to hear truth
The eyes caught on the shiny reflection
Another product to sell
GIANTS compared to a majestic fish
Chasing after a fifty-dollar lures
Only to be put on the butcher block
Getting ripped
Getting tore
Another Giants joy.
The mind
Playing games
Fooling the world, of self-made ideas
Like that of a plant
That won't hold in ground
The universe
Sitting in the stall
Reading the who's who
in Giant world now
A soft grunt is heard
Followed by a splash
falling from the sky
To find a happy recipient
"SHIT REALLY DOES FLY!"
The Being contemplates
While sitting on the curb
An arguing Hippopotamus
That floats through the air

Gocni Schindler

Laughing Penguins without a home
Wobble as they chase each other's tails
Talk of love resounds
as dead birds crash to the ground
Two talking Kitties discussing politics
Who we kidding, it turns into a claw brawl
While a Dog bitches about the local team
Giants continually pass along
The world is in tears
The greed of Giant monsters
Has everything obscured
Imagine how foolish we look
To those that are small
While no one will ask
Who owns the WORLD Now?

SANITY VIA CRITIQUES

In the wonder of the mystery
The mystery of this layman's mind
Rests the conclusive response
of chance, risk, sacrifice
Endurance to last this dance
Without putting an end to it all
Acknowledgment of the knowledge
From pointed understanding of good patience
Steadfastness, a solid determination
To strive, to fight, for something that never really comes
Fulfilled, not one off- chasing in the playground
Worth more than anything earmarked
By the simpleton's eye
Solid, yet simple individual
Self-proclaimed such orchestrations
Some, written words
Laid upon parchment paper
Amazing, how the deepest pulchritude
Can capture the pneuma
In the instance of simplicity as if two pieces of metal
Easily fused with the strongest of bond
Through a little heat
Some basic science
Not to come undone
So, does it seem logically true
Two pneuma's could share same in possibility
My critiques shall argue
That in the essence of my deep
Conducive mind
I have lost my damn marbles
Look, they're scattered across the ground
Seeing my mind
Is like the ocean

Something ALWAYS new
To discover
I tend to disagree
Essence of discovery
Seeking what one has willed
As the eye is blind
To what the voice does say
With the wind, to carry home
Messages, what the sane call
Timely insane illusions
What was whispered
Finally appears
Then notably, when the eye is finally freed
Beholding what was missed!
The great mystery
Is something prodigious
Copious rather
Something affluently rare
To the reader
This madness
Yet for the talebearer,
Something magical!
A note of ebullient affection
Of this tale
The clueless wails at the reading
Confusion is meant for many
While though, the flower of
Mystery only blooms
For the one who tends it.
It is the mystery
It's something that this
pneuma knows to Be

Tripping Balls

Always, always

Better inside you

Always, always

Always, always

Better, inside you!

CAPTAIN ASS HAT

SHITDATE: Many light years away.
TIME: 13:13
LOCATION: Another cesspool called SPACE
YEAR: 3131 give or take
Is this my mind, spinning outta control?
Oh wait, the gosh damn ships about to blow!
I evacuated the crew. Give it a good Check!
A female androidish, kind of whorish
voice crackles over the digicom.
CRRRAAAACCCCKKKKKLLLLLE
"Captain, blow is an incorrect term, the ship is going to Melt Down!"
EVA, my beautiful computer, that got us into this mess
It's going to blow!
CRRRAAAACCCCKKKKKLLLLLE
"Excuse me Captain, it was your orders that got us into this
situation; this MELT DOWN is your fault and now, I'm going to cease to exist!"
EVA be quiet, I'm recording my log!

CRRRAAAACCCCKKKKKLLLLLE
"Captain, I would like the log to be accurate, to be precise, I am not at fault!"
EVA, who is the captain?
CRRRAAAACCCCKKKKKLLLLLE
"Captain Ass Hat."
EVA, who is Captain Ass Hat?
CRRRAAAACCCCKKKKKLLLLLE
"Captain Ass Hat is you, Sir!"
Great, now that we have that settled, please silence your

microphone box.
CRRRAAAACCCCKKKKKLLLLLE
"Captain, I speak from a voice integration system!"
EVA, I would like you to shut the fuck up, go cook me up a pie or something!
CRRRAAAACCCCKKKKKLLLLLE
"Captain, I will not be talked to like this! You don't ever talk to me like this!"
EVA please! *********
******SILENCE*******
******SILENCE*******
******SILENCE*******
Finally, so where was I, oh yeah!
All that remains on this mission of
Doom is of course, yours truly.
CAPTAIN ASS HAT
Yeah, well, if the ship is gotta go down
Let's go down in a blaze of glory.
Just, not with me!
I didn't purchase the notion of the Cap goes down with the
Ship. What a bunch of bullshit that is!
I'm a paid employee
Dying, wasn't in the job description.
Onto another thought
Wonder what my counter parts on grandma earth are up to?
Probably hanging out, sharing smiles with some sweat.
Some spit, a little wet in the pants, perhaps.
They all drink a bit too much
I'd kill for a nice drink of that Crank Craft
There she is again
I try to remember the touch of her lips!
OK, Captain, why in the hell is this
going to be the last thought?

CRRRAAAACCCCKKKKKLLLLLE!
"Captain!"
Yes, EVA, my loyal ship computer!
CRRRAAAACCCCKKKKKLLLLLE
"Captain I'm shutting down power to extend the time to meltdown!"
This ship is going to blow, EVA!
CRRRAAAACCCCKKKKKLLLLLE
"Captain, the ship is going to go into a meltdown phase before it detonates."
Shit, EVA, meltdown, blow, who gives a shit?
Why is it always an argument with you women?
You're a damn computer, still you argue!
CRRRAAAACCCCKKKKKLLLLLE
"Captain, I am merely explaining what will take place!"
GREAT, PERFECT! Don't you have something else to do?
CRRRAAAACCCCKKKKKLLLLLE
"Captain, it is futile for me to do much seeing the probability of survival is zero percent, I'm going to die, Captain! All because of you, this is your fault, Captain."

Ok, yep, great, EVA, you are going to die!
Now, let me get back to going over my thoughts!
CRRRAAAACCCCKKKKKLLLLLE
"Yes, Captain, you selfish bastard!"
Oh, bother me! Where was I?
Oh, yes, my last thought
What I did or didn't do! How the relationship wasn't saved.
Seriously, what in the mad hell is wrong with me?
I must just be mad insane, with dried cum on the brain!
Ha, ha, yeah, I'm on a ship that is about to BLOW.

Tripping Balls

CRAAAAACCCCKKKKKLLLLLE
"Melt Down Captain!"
Grinding teeth with a thank you EVA!!
Think, Captain, yeah, think!
What about your fast V-spectra speeder?
Sitting in the docking garage
Just collecting millennium dust
Last time, oh, so nice
Took that beauty out on a beat flight
Clocked out at 480 Light cycles per minute
Speed, putting your balls in your ass
That's how mom use to say it
Gosh damn it
Yeah, oh, wait, yeah, that's right
That little green bastard is
Riding my V-spectra speeder
With my former wench.
His balls, getting sucked into her ass.
Wait, SHIT!
Yeah, OK, what about all the times at Plan Disaster?
Ah shit, that was the place we met.
I see it won't matter cause the warning sirens
Warning sirens, just screaming around me
EVA, shut off the warning sirens for fucks sake!
CRRAAAAACCCCKKKKLLLLE
"Yes, Captain!"
Look at all these pretty lights
Blazing, in a glorious red.
It's like being at some cheap
Chronic Stripper disco underground
The whore district is here!
CRRRAAAACCCCKKKKKLLLLLE
"Captain, this is the central control center of this ship. It was never labeled a whore district!"

EVA, if I could, I would turn you into a whore, then perhaps, just perhaps, you would SHUT THE FUCK UP!
CRRRAAAACCCCKKKKKLLLLLE
"Captain..."
SHUT UP
CRRRAAAACCCCKKKKKLLLLLE
"Captain."
SHUT UP
CRRRAAAACCCCKKKKKLLLLLE!
"CAP..."
SHUT UP, EVA!
Damn it, once again, where was I?
Yes, the lights.
Fleet command sure didn't spring any credits
For these piles of crap!
I mean, look, this one here that isn't even flashing.
Ah, what the hell?
It's not like you can see what I can.
Really, what's the point in blowing some good credits on lights that are about to be vaporized when the SHIP BLOWS!

CRRRAAAACCCCKKKKKLLLLLE
"Captain....
EVA, Shh!
CRRRAAAACCCCKKKKKLLLLLE
"Captain...."
EVA shut the hell up!
CRRRAAAACCCCKKKKKLLLLLE
"Captain!!...I'd appreciate a better form of dialogue, innocent children will read this someday. Captain Ass Hat, got it! Innocent Children!"
Any way's there is EVA again
Miss Ship Computer, telling me what I already know!

CRRRAAAACCCCKKKKKLLLLLE
"CAPTAIN, Two Minutes and thirty seconds remains till
core meltdown occurs!"
EVA, you bitch, I know it's going to blow
CRRRAAAACCCCKKKKKLLLLLE
"Captain, I was simply informing you the time remaining till Melt-Down occurs. Two Minutes and twenty-three seconds!"
EVA, can I have One minute of thoughts
On my love that left me
DO YOU THINK I CAN HAVE THAT EVA?!?
CRRRAAAACCCCKKKKKLLLLLE
"My voice needs to be heard Captain!"
EVA you're a damn box of bits, written with obvious shit code
CRRRAAAACCCCKKKKKLLLLLE
"That was so mean to say, I can't believe you said that Captain!"
Blaa, blaa, blaa, EVA
Thinking about it!
Wicked bitch, how could you do this to me?
Took my dog when she left too
Stole my V-spectra speeder,
Left me, Left me, Captain Ass Hat, me!
For that three-foot, short sack of green alien anus lick
That Scum sucker from the outer rings, Saff
I mean, how the hell was I supposed to compete,
with a three Foot, short, green alien thing that
has two organs of pleasure?
Yeah, yeah, sure he can dance.
Sure, he can sing, but come the fuck on!
I AM A CAPTAIN OF THE ANAL-FRIED FEDERATION!

Yeah, I remember, when I came home for the weekend after
The Expedition to the Scrotum Twuatdrip.
Came home all excited, like a good Captain would
The house, always so nice, she always picked up like a
Good little house wife. This time, the house was dark!
Walking in to the smell of spices
That usually meant, go directly into the bedroom for fun.
It was our little signal for passion night.
So, I remember, happily, walking into the bedroom.
I didn't notice stepping on alien underpants
Then it was
What do my wondering eyes see?
CRRRAAAACCCCKKKKKLLLLLE
"Captain, how does anyone know what you see?"
EVA, this is my own conversation, I'm telling a story here!
Can a man just talk to reflect his mind?
His damn life
CRRRAAAACCCCKKKKKLLLLLE
"Captain, it doesn't compute. How can anyone
see what you see! No one is here on the ship with you!"
No, dip shit EVA, I'm talking to my damn self!
CRRRAAAACCCCKKKKKLLLLLE
"Captain, it still doesn't compute, moron!"
EVA, you bitch, you want to have an argument on this?
Just follow your damn orders, get the cannon ready!
CRRRAAAACCCCKKKKKLLLLLE
"Yes, Captain, what order?"
So where was I?
Huh, EVA, I told you to get the cannon ready, to shoot this
jolly red ass into space. Pointed in the direction of rotten crotch grandma EARTH!

Tripping Balls

CRRRAAAACCCCKKKKKLLLLLE
"Captain, you never gave me that command!"
EVA, my cynical little pile of scrap, I specifically commanded you to get the cannon ready!
CRRRAAAACCCCKKKKKLLLLLE
"Captain, you never gave such a command. If you ask nicely
maybe I'll proceed to getting the cannon ready to shoot you into space, not that you will survive or anything."
Yes, EVA, please, would you be so kind TO GET THE DAMN CANNON READY!
CRRRAAAACCCCKKKKKLLLLLE
"Captain you don't have to shout!"
Once again
So where was I?
Ahh, no dip shit, it wasn't no god damn man in a red suit
Leaving gifts under a VR Tree
It was that alien scum Saff, all three feet short of him
Working on my mate, it was more of a sick pounding
She sure liked it rough.
I was stuck in the door, just stuck
Eyes just lost, my bed bounced
Saff rode her as if she was some god damn ride.
Saff, yeah, what did he say his name meant.
"Seconds Aren't for Free!"
Shit, I can see his little Three foot
short ass, dancing on what was my bed....
MY GOD DAMN BED!!!!
With his two organs of pleasure, bouncing around.
His green ass face, smirking along to his illustrious songs.
"My name is Saff, how do you do?
I'm here pleasing your woman
in all the glorious ways
you could never do!

do-do-do
cause I got me that extra part.
La-Di-da
When it's all said, and done
I'll be kicking it
with your dog, too!
Yeah, O, yeah,
My name is Saff!
Who the hell are you?"
ARGH, Fucker!
Captain Ass Hat is my damn name!
Captain of the bastard ship
in the ANAL-FRIED FEDERATION
Yeah, blah, blah, blah, Fuck you, Saff.
I should have blasted his ass
With my ICOCK Ray!
Saff, what a cock mud sucker!
Well, as I try to not go too deep into
thought on this, but low and behold
CRRRAAAACCCCKKKKKLLLLLE
"Captain, I did the calculations, Saff is an Insextual
being from the planet Sacknutlucious, near the outer
rings. They're a colony style insect
with socialistic ideologies. They enjoy the arts,
music, theater and can bare roughly 300 young in one
mating! Calculations show, that if human DNA and
Insextual DNA cross, it would be a being with super
sexual abilities, that will fancy the arts."
Its sounds like they would be gay to me, EVA,
thank you for that useful information!
Please everyone, give EVA a standing ovation
For her wise input once again!
CRRRAAAACCCCKKKKKLLLLLE
"Captain, it doesn't compute, who will be giving me a

standing ovation? There are no other life forms on the ship
except for you. Soon, I too will be terminated, thank you!"
Oh great, we're here again
CRRRAAAACCCCKKKKKLLLLLE
"The ship hasn't moved Captain!"
I'm going to rip the damn hair outta my head!
CRRRAAAACCCCKKKKKLLLLLE
"Captain, do you need a haircut? I can send in the robot!"
Did I do something wrong in a former life?
CRRRAAAACCCCKKKKKLLLLLE
"Captain, the probability of a former life is one and 64 billion. You are screwed by my calculations.
EVA, please for the love of it just shut the bleep UP!

CRRRAAAACCCCKKKKKLLLLLE
"Yes, Captain! Did you still want the robot for a haircut?"
EVA, did you just bleep me?
CRRRAAAACCCCKKKKKLLLLLE
"Captain, I've had enough of your vulgarity!"
Oh, you better not bleep, bleep, bleep, bleep, bleep, EVA!
 Bleep, bleep blip-pity bleep EVA!
EVA!!!!
Does it seem like I will be having time for a damn hair cut?
CRRRAAAACCCCKKKKKLLLLLE
"I would like to answer your question, Captain. But you told me to shut the bleep up!"
EVA please just ready the canon!
CRRRAAAACCCCKKKKKLLLLLE
"No, I was told to shut the bleep up!"

EVA, please, I'm sorry! Under a little stress here.
CRRRAAAACCCCKKKKKLLLLLE
"Yes, Captain!"
Thank you, EVA,
Now back to my thoughts
Seriously, is this going to be my last thought?
A woman, for reasons unknown to me,
Daring to even give a moment of thought
A last thought to boot.
To BOOT, to boot, to boot
what kind of wanker says that lame ass word?
To BOOT!
CRRRAAAACCCCKKKKKLLLLLE
"Captain, it appears you say that kind of wanker word."
AHHHH, just shoot me
Oh, EVA dear, what time remains?
CRRRAAAACCCCKKKKKLLLLLE
"Captain, calculations indicate you should
stick your head between your legs, give those
two robin's eggs you call nuts a big kiss, then slap your
ass goodbye, for there is a few minutes left. Would you
like me to count down to the end?"
EVA, you bitch, your countdown to extinction
Has been all over the damn place!
What exactly is the point in counting down?
Get the cannon prepared to launch.
I'm just going to look out into space while I wet myself!
Hey you! It's Captain Ass Hat, did you hear that?
Of course, you didn't, you can't hear what you read.
So, to inform you, I just slapped myself senseless!
CRRRAAAACCCCKKKKKLLLLLE!
"Captain, why are you slapping yourself?
Do you need a sedative?"
No, EVA, I don't need a sedative! It's bleep stress relief.
CRRRAAAACCCCKKKKKLLLLLE

Tripping Balls

"Captain, would you like me to summons the psychiatrist
program, so you can talk to someone?"
EVA, the ship is going to bleep blow into oblivion
CRRRAAAACCCCKKKKKLLLLLE
"Captain, the ship is in meltdown mode!"
Melt down mode, blow up mode,
it's like she's pregnant.
She's with child, no bitch, she's knocked the bleep up.
What's the gosh damn argument here, EVA?
And quit bleep my bleep dialogue!
Shits the same thing!
CRRRAAAACCCCKKKKKLLLLLE
"Captain, I'm just trying to help,
your stress levels have elevated exponentially!"
EVA, start helping me, by not helping!

CRRRAAAACCCCKKKKKLLLLLE
"Yes, Captain!"
Alright, let's get things together here.
That little rodent, her three feet package of insect chops
Can eat, my dry shitted, polka dotted space shorts.
OK, well, it's time to put this space suit on.
Going to attempt to launch myself
outta one of the proton cannons.
Or wait, is it neutron cannon?
Shit, does it matter what it is?
CRRRAAAACCCCKKKKKLLLLLE
"Captain, the correct term is a Prorgasim Cannon!"
Oh, well thank you, EVA
For giving me an education on what the hell it is
Doesn't everyone feel smarter now?
You, there, yes, you reading.
Don't you feel just slightly more intelligent
knowing what the cannon is?

Don't answer, hate to think you're going crazy.
CRRRAAAACCCCKKKKKLLLLLE
"Captain there is no other life forms to feel smarter on this ship!"
Of course, there is EVA, they're all around us.
CRRRAAAACCCCKKKKKLLLLLE
"Captain, I believe you are suffering
from last moment of life syndrome. I feel I should initiate the psychiatrist program!"
Stress, who me? What stress? Ha-ha are you kidding!
Prorgasim cannon who gives a shit!
As long as it shoots me into
space before this Cum wagon blows into oblivion.
CRRRAAAACCCCKKKKKLLLLLE
"Captain, this ship is in a Meltdown mode."
Please tell me, what the hell did I do to deserve this?
EVA, that's all that matters, isn't it? You're right, I'm wrong!
CRRRAAAACCCCKKKKKLLLLLE
"Captain, I am right, thank you for acknowledging that!"
Did some feminist scum program you?
You're a hateful bitch.
It's funny, this ship is just like another woman in my life to just get up, to just run with a tucked tail and all.
Hell, maybe it's me,
maybe I'm the problem?
DEEEEEP THOUGHT!
CRRRAAAACCCCKKKKKLLLLLE
"Captain, statistics state that you are 90% the Problem!"
EVA, who the hell asked you?
Na, I'm the complete package. Can't ever be me because I'm
Captain Ass Hat!!
CRRRAAAACCCCKKKKKLLLLLE
"Why isn't it asshole? That would be more fitting."

Tripping Balls

That wasn't nice, EVA.
Well, this time, it's my turn
while I say adieus, to just toss the union band on the floor.
Run a few programs on this bitch of a ship
Aim me in the direction of grandma earth
then slide myself in this tube of risk, then poof, away I go.
Feeling a bit like a dick in the hole!
Open the door, then up the shaft I go!
Gives real meaning to a rectal exam.
I'm like the good Doctor's finger
Shit, this tube is a tight fit, should've used a little lube!
Ha, ha, got me enough air to last a week or two.
Then, set the homing beacon on the suit "BOOM" out the
mother humping door I go, back to grandma Earth.

CRRRAAAACCCCKKKKKLLLLLE
"Captain, you have a survival rate of 10 percent and a detection probability of 33 Percent. Odds are you will die from suffocation before being rescued!"
EVA, you bitch! I can do 10 percent!
It's been a pleasure being with you, EVA
Now fire this bad boy!
CRRRAAAACCCCKKKKKLLLLLE
"Captain, Firing in three, two, one, it's been a pleasure to
serve you, good bye, Captain Ass Hat. Thank you for killing me! May you have a good death!"
EVA, SHUT THE BLEEE! Oh shiiiiiiiiiiiiiiiiiiiiiiiit
AHHHHHHHHHHHHHHHH shiiiiiiiiiiiiiiiiiiiiiiiiit!
I'm out, HAHA I made it!
 There is my ship, BLOWING UP into oblivion
CRRRAAAACCCCKKKKKLLLLLE

"Captain, the ship is Me.............."
EVA? EVAaaaaaa!!! EVA is gone. I will miss her she was a good little computer!
Made it out just in time!
Hit this distress beacon.
I will make this.
I'm coming back for my V-spectra speeder
For my dog, I will make it.
Captain Ass Hat always delivers!
Going to kick Saff directly in his extra package, launching
Him back into space where he belongs!
Going to show that I am still the Captain!
Watch and see............Captain Ass Hat
Signing off!

3:13

In the reality of beauty
She is, Everything
Looking back
The light was glistening
There was, WOMAN
Mother to a kingdom
Who is named, no self-worth
Light consumed by darkness
Sorrow, the face she wore
Down kisser was the path she rode
Lies, lies, deceptive tasks kept her
From what she was meant to be
Truth, evades the brightest of mind
With the greatest of ease
Flashing bright lights
Mind's movie player
Only viewing lies
Time travels onward, the sun's wicked curse
Moons move shadows
Scattering
Trample down whisper kisser's path
Positive remarks
Like hooks for rocks
Never taking hold
Dark little words
Parsimonious really
Wonder is life passing along
Before a make-believe, QUEEN
Discovers never what is real
True self only ever made whole
when lies are no more
while the time reads 3:13
Now she is out the door

John Smith

John Smith
He sure was smart
Enlightened
Gifted
Intelligent
John Smith
Had an Inner Flame
Native was his breed in English name
It was the hunger
That constantly burned
John Smith
The wild one
A torch out of control
Just burn, you bastard, burn
Melt it away
Remnants, items, toss them in
All fake with no meaning
Nothing- All based on fantasy
Eyes opened
Truth makes one
ANNIHILATED
John Smith
Water; life's juice
Washes mud, the dirty filth away
Dirty little fish
Swim fish, just SWIM
John Smith
A local guy
Grew up tough
Hard edged
Tested, tried, true
Gifted with off the earth gifts from the wolf

Tripping Balls

Sure, he was blinder than a bat
He had some luck
He had no hope in sight
Another lost soul
Born on loser's road
John Smith
Didn't give two shit's
Lived for the day
A moment in given time
Thought of everyone else
Never, not ever
Seeking for self
Looking at death with love
Death seemed to be found
Finding assentator's, users, talkers and thieves
Companionship in groups of brutes
Living not for the day, more like the minute
John Smith
Intelligent, not today though
They tossed him off a bridge
He was in too deep
Money, they would say
More, way, way more
Than he bargained for
John Smith
Swimming down a river
Swimming like a fish
All for some serving wench
Fish like asking the tough questions
"How do you swim, John Smith?"
John Smith
He can't swim
All those times at the river
Being kids
Not once, not ever one time

Gocni Schindler

Did he swim
John Smith was scared of the deep
Sink, John Smith, sink
His eyes, must be blank
The release
That lease of air
Bubbles go to the surface
Returned to the sky god
Back to the crow
Shit is only leased, he would say
Bye, bye, John Smith
Bye, Bye
Don't worry not one fret
It's alright
PEOPLE DIE
John Smith

SLEEP

Sleep, that confounded theater of pleasure
This human body, longs for it
I'm like a hunter
In a blackened forest
Sleep, that prized buck
Always cruelly eluding me
Then, as I break the final horizon
I only mark my sights to assimilate
A doe beholding
Something I dare not kill
Two small innocent peering eyes
From a fawn, looking, peering out, helplessly
Under the safety of its mother
An image that not even I'd dare separate
The image dissipates
I pretend to sleep
Open these eyes
I wasn't asleep with this mind
Racing with thoughts of life
A path that seems to grip me
It could be this pain
Swelling in my hip
Arousing me
My body longs for some meds
That I dare not give
Doctors with their meds
Making me, dependent; making me, weak
Though, that pain slowly diminishes
As I lay awake, staring at a blackened ceiling
I can't help but think
Thoughts of beauty
That marvelous creature
She was another name in disguise

Can't have her master finding out
Sharing her, a heinous crime
Still, a society filled with fairy tales
My eyes focused upon my darkened ceiling
As if I was at a picture show
Holding my popcorn that I can't eat
Drinking from a non-existent
Nice glass of spiked iced tea
The curtains draw, the ceiling opens
A bright light burst forth
Lighting my face, feeling the warmth
Smiling with anticipation
As if! As if in a vintage age of cinematography
The screen crackles black with white
My eyes lay siege to the famous
Three, two, one
Then a picture is shown
My mind like a child
At five AM Christmas time
A gift under the tree
My senses, heighten with sheer glee
It's as if heaven itself is before me
I see the man in white
The one, who created light
Though, not a man in human term
Yet has a gift for me
NO NEVER IN THIS DAZE
Something of beauty
least at the time
She beheld me special
With adornments Laid out for me
In her skin, nakedness
Complete vulnerability
Scenes unfold
Female creature more orphic

Tripping Balls

Than anything ever recorded
Her every detail laid in perfect array
She adorns such black thick hair
Those lips, best thing to kiss
Her smell, Fuck, do I miss
Eyes that sparkle a crystal blue
This mind is gone
Maybe I'll touch myself
As a sheet of paper is blank
'Til the hand takes the pen
Laying hold, gripping, filling it with an honest ink
Glorious refinement
Turning thoughts in thy darkest of circumstance
I'm paralyzed in reality
To thoughts most dynamic
Though dynamic
Dynamic as a word
No, No, No- that description
Doesn't even measure true an image
An image that takes the worst of frowns
Making the very best of smiles
In times of the gravest of incidents
I'm in love- the injustice abounds
Falling off the world above
What a thought can have
To the creative mind
Pictures for the eye
Those passions held together
With fervent emotions
Togetherness with the ultimate
Sensation of life
As if the cold of winter was on my face
My breath takes the form
Invisible showing before me
Her warmth embraces

The world covered in snow, hell bent to be frozen
Trap it for all time, never to share the moment
My attire doesn't match the climate
This feeble yet effective body
Turns cold as ice- I'm freezing to death
Her hand grips my pen
She makes me warm again
Brings me back to life
Takes me at nothing
Accepts me for everything
Laying hold rags from riches
Essence of thought
Turning this winter storm into tropics
We melt, one we become
What I see belongs to me
I dare not share it with a greedy world
So very undeserving
Yet, in the terminal state of time
Endurance do I start to lose
I long to share this one reality
Though, her master must never find out
Will make all dead from deeds done
I am, the bee, penetrating a spring time flower
Making ready to bloom
Only sharing her beauty with a few
In aspect, though, I am selfish
Holding dear to these thoughts
Valuing them more than self
In manner like a sculptor
Valuing his many tools
Yet, only one is precious
Never to be lost, never to be shared
This very notion of thought
Having more notoriety
Than that of some dick named Matt

Tripping Balls

Mr. Big time distinguished public super star
This thought, this magic
Could sail to the end of the world
So effortlessly prevailed all the challenges
On a raging sea
This thought is what will help me to sleep
I love her above self, biggest mistake
So, unfortunate
Now shit, can I finally sleep
I'm paralyzed
Refusing what doesn't work
Meds of course

Gocni Schindler

Old in the Rain

As I peer out my window
Looking out to the pouring rain
I see an old man walking
To his mailbox
What I mistake for rain on his face
In reality is tears
Tears that fall to the ground like rain
Salty little drops
That mix so well with pain
The sky, darkened from the retreated sun
That went to rest Its weary head
The earth blankets the sky with those
Glorious darkened clouds in spite
The moon attempting to trickle the earth
With an ounce of Shallow light
Evil showing faces upon the smog
laughing at his pain
Outside he stands
Face gazing to heaven not afraid
The rain gracefully splashes
Off his wrinkled face
Drops trickling off an edged chin
raising old arms
winds gusting against him, yet he stands
Mail blowing out violently from steady grips
Rain drops crashing
Upon his hands
Between his fingers
cold drops squish in his clenched fist
He turns slow
Like most geriatrics do, I assume
Lightning striking tree limbs
another brilliant light

Tripping Balls

While giving its glorious
Thunderous delight
Under the powerful sky
Does he stand, fearless
With the story of life
only to share it with
Emptiness of night
The winds gust's harder
Nature is moved
It's cold, wet
I look on confused
The thought in my head
Shit, should I do something
To my dismay the old man is smiling.
softly closing his eyes
He spins
Then in my amazement
I see a shadowy figure appear
That amazingly resembles a female
The old man still circles
As he reaches out to take hold
Knowing exactly where the shadow is
The shadowy figure's hair flows
In the wind like silk
old fingers touch a darkened face
Hands aged in time
Embracing the cheek
My mind in a state of shock
I can only imagine what he feels
Cold, yet loved, like newborn to mother's breast
The shadow tilts its darkened head
To embrace those old gentle hands
Feeling Every luscious detail
Wrinkled creases upon tender strength
Beautiful to the touch

The shadows hands lifting
To hold his
Cold, yet soft fingers
Fingers searching each other's
Telling their own story
Hands that melt into the soul
Two faces embrace
My eyes take hold
My Mind simply lost in what I cannot ascertain
Her hair permeates his senses
His nose presses against her essence
His chest moves
Taking in what I assume to be heaven
His eyes open
He looks into her eyes
A glimmering green
Burst forth in light
Bright emeralds in the night
Showing every minute detail of her face
Stunningly beautiful
Her smile brings forth a new-found hope
It incapacitates his soul
They move in circles
Enchanting dancers that spin
Not one care
The rain goes unnoticed for she's here
Eyes locking
Her spirit light, captivating
They laugh as kids
Innocent lovers
His mouth to hers
Her nose against his
His forehead, pressed against hers
Tucking her head under his chin
Togetherness breathtaking

Those things, taken for granted
They invigorate them
My eyes, fixed at what is
Extremely rare
Something taken for granted in
A world lost in selfishness
Nothing that should be forgotten
A treasure everyone wants
But only the few obtain
Here she is
In her glorious beauty once again
They are one.
The earth in wickedness screeches
As if to say
ENOUGH!
He looks at her in that saddened state
For once again the time is nigh
She gently places her finger on his lips
Her head turns towards him with compassion
I witness what her lips say
"I am always here!"
Her smile
Shinning like the sun
Purest of love
He closes his eyes
As the lightning flashes
As the thunder rages
His eyes slowly opening
With childlike anticipation
only to find
He is once again alone in the rain
She's gone
His best friend, soul mate
a vision dissipates
the shadow fades

His head falls long
For only memories remain
A lifetime of love
Vanished with the wind
The mail disappears in a whirlwind
His lips quiver soft words
"I don't want to be here!"
Staggering his way back home
Home that brought him joy
now, just an empty tomb
Full of memories.
A life of love
That is all but gone

Tripping Balls

Kaboooooom

Holding a sign was this dude
The sign stated:
GOD IS COMING
TO JUDGE
THE QUICK AND THE DEAD
ITS TIME TO REPENT
Suddenly
The sky blackened in mid-day
Eyes face the heavens
FLASH
Let there be light, in glorious perception
Those beautiful eyes
Obliterated
Erased from natures sights
Crimson is the color
Sky turned dead
LIFE
Crashing, Broken, Halted
Opened wide thy bowels of hell
Fire filled the air
Demons dancing in the flame
Boiling in man's plasm
Ripping, tearing, no escape
None are spared
INSTANTLY
He was raptured
Only his shadow remained
In light, Darkness has no place
In a mountain is a man
Who pushed a button
His sign
THE END

God and man were sitting in the bar drinking till good and drunk. God told man, if you don't stop talking politics I'm going to wipe you from the land. Man, said to God, don't worry about wiping us off the land. We got this, it's called a nuclear bomb.

JOURNEY WITH ME

Is it a journey into hysteria?
A never ending
Problematic
Course into useless rhetoric behavior
Between mind
Between body
Between the unseen spirit
If I were to be given
A chance
At removing the unseen events
In the uncontrollable future
The world for me would be all green grass
The never-ending possibilities
Of the best damn life, ever!
But, to the ultimate joy of others
While your face is in the mud of life
And others walk over it like a door mat
It is, with great regret
That in order for others to go ahead
There is a few
That must
Oh, as they say, be put down
Now, I know that in the cruelty of life
This unfortunate tale
Is told through the useless rambling
Of a historic idiot
But the truth is always told
The facts are that nothing is easy
The children of life
They never seem to go anywhere
But to the bottom
Like a fish swimming in the water
With a rock tied to its fin

No matter how hard it tries to swim
The uncontrollable end
Living its remaining moments
At the bottom
While enjoying the faint reflection
Of the sun's rays shinning off the surface
Now, on the other hand
At times
There are a few
That manage to come from the wreckage
Fulfilling somewhat complete life
Although we rarely have the honor of meeting these people
For does one ever take the time to look down
When your eye is up?
Does one ever take the eye off the bottom?
To look at the top?
Do you see the person next to you?
And wonder.
What have you seen?
What have you done?
If I could borrow your eye
What would I see?
Is your black white, while my white is black?
What love have you seen or pain have your eyes endured
If I could borrow your hand
What would I feel?
The ear is a treasure to its own
If I had your ear, what could I hear?
Would I hear the heartbeat?
Of someone you loved
Or the faint breath that you give
While smelling your love's hair?
Would the waves crash sound the same?

Tripping Balls

Oh, what is it to be me
That would desire me to be you
What if you could just strip away?
All the material items
Possessions and titles
Clothing and cars
Homes in their fancy
What would we have?
Nakedness surrounded by mediocrity
What would a man be without his wealth?
What would be a woman without her worry?
Maybe we need to have a top and a bottom
Or men and women alike
Would just go into a stir of madness
I am here, you are there
The separation is important
Maybe it's not
Be like the children
Jumping and shouting like little kids do
They don't see nakedness
They don't see wrong or right
They believe and see what they want
Look mommy
I'm chasing a butterfly
Now watch me fly
A faint giggle with bright wide eyes
My house is a castle
And the neighbor girl is a princess
And I am defending against the giant dragon
Maybe, just maybe
We, the adults, are the dragons
Who long to steal the imagination of the children!
Isn't that what happened to us
Where did you go, you that use to make believe?
Paul once said

I put away my childish things
Maybe, the creator never wanted us like that
Didn't Jesus say to enter the kingdom
You have to be like little children
Was he speaking to grown men?
Why do we fret over what we have or don't have?
What title must we obtain to get our disdain
While looking for our place
We miss our calling
Looking under rocks for our gold
While we should have been plucking stars
Why do we try to live?
When our time is near!
What if, to go home
You had to go to your childhood
Watch the elderly that have lost their mind
Or did they lose their mind?
Maybe we lost our mind in our obsession
For greatness, when greatness is to be young and free
Ah, free
What is that word that is so loosely spoken?
Are you free as you say?
I bet not!
Slave to your goals
Your dreams
Your desires
Slave to your society with all its establishments
Slave or free- is it a choice?
Or something you're born with
More like
A dash of free and a dash of slave
To make the pie just right
Welcome to the bakery of your desire
I will cook you up a pie
Of your wildest desires

Tripping Balls

Now eat it up
Isn't that good
Yummy in the tummy little Timmy
Like a sweet cherry
'Til it's sour in the stomach
Cherry, just doesn't seem so good
Don't forget to spit out the seed
Enjoy
Well with this
I give the one finger salute to life and say
In that monotone voice
Farewell, good night

S-12 A-16 M-08

When I buried him
Buried something with him
Awoken, something else
It was as if
The whole thing
Just a hellish dream
While being stuck in reality
Time of unpleasantness
I look back
I know every minute
Yet I wonder
Did it even really happen
Do I really exist?
Is any of this REAL
I'D LOVE TO RIP THE CURTAIN DOWN
Expose this damn lie
Fractional work of bullshit fiction
We call life
Life, is just a goddamn lie
In the sight of loss,
one only has the bottom
to enjoy the light from
From the bottom,
where roots dig deep into ground.
Roots to build again
To climb the rocks
Getting back to the ground

Tripping Balls

Voices in my head, give me advice!
Voices to the fray, that I could be insane.

Something Nice

Wrote this for a broad once
It sucked, that's why it's here
Enjoy it, she didn't
When you check in it might be coy
if someone left you a proclamation
of things to read
This little note that may just say
what a wonderful place this is to play
Now, that if one might
by chance, happen along this wee bit path
To find such a one as thee
to see her reading with delight
a wonderful note to give her flight
that does uplift on golden wings
to bring new height that life can be
A never-ending place of congruous tranquility
So, then you will see
that not all things are what they seem
Then, wouldn't life be unfaltering indeed
I'd like to date you, pick you up at eight?
No, you're weird!

MOTHER

One that always looks back
It's in the mirror
When doing that hair
Beautify that face
There it is
When brushing teeth
Damn reflection
When all you see
What use to be
This one bothering the hell out of mommy
Life thus far
Standing alone, Hands raised
Wondering, what has become of her?
Dreams for a dreamer
Naive is one of her traits
Use to believe
Fictitious characters
That he was going to save the day
Holding the blue hand from a corpse
If success was measured in failure
Then mother would be very successful
Looking self in the mirror
Once having a dream
Such a great speech
Dreams come with price tags
Nothing is free!
That was for mommy
Try hard to deny people
What they want from jealousy
Truth, when you deal with absolutes
Talking with the sperm donor
Telling her that he was great things
Please Save the serenade of bull shit

For a lesser pupil, she would say
Knowing exactly what things are
What mother is
Don't hide in cheap talk
No phony masquerades
Truth; when talking
Mother knows not!
Watching the body monitoring those eyes
Eyes for those who never lie
A talent, a curse
Mother monitors it well
Problems one would surmise
Mother having more problems than most
Just that she can easily hide
Most wouldn't even now
Pills easily remove depression
Defeat tosses her back
Into a huge regression
Self-examination, filled frustration
Childhood trauma doesn't seem to go away
Many reasons, so many
Seeking purposely- destroy any relationship
With man, Mommy knowing best
Truth is like gold, dig to be honest
In mother's mind
The cowardice of woman
She was the monster Mommy warned about
Though; always its justified in actions
Filled with excuses
Truth shines through
Damn Monster!
Woman, another blame game
Unending escape into reality
Her own disillusioned reality
The pseudo reality

Tripping Balls

The World sees Only
What Mommy gives
Perfect painting all worn well
A great act
Don't worry mommy
Eyes see all, quite well
Look close, tension in the voice
Mommy's body language
Watch those gates to the soul!
Lost down hell's road
A new persona
Mommy hides it well

WORLD OF MAKE BELIEVE

Times, upon times has the world turned
Turned, to never learn from what has been before
Before, that broken fictional door
Door, to another work
Art, of those who live on the curb
Curb sights, simple plain art
World filled with zombies
Aimlessly walking past
Past those eyes, never looking
Down, upon human parasites not worth the frown
Parasites, who come waving
Waving in their invisibility
Invisibility like a clown
Clown with items to sell
MARKETING, BUSINESS, PROFITS
Purchase a ticket
It's a movie, take a seat
Grab the popcorn
Take hold of XXX soda
We got some drama
Another Jesus said action scene
 "The world has always had the broken down."
Eyes too fixed upon fictional clouds
A white cross, cast upon the slain
 "RED BLOOD"
Expensive items, rich wear the crowns
A woman sits upon the ground
An infant upon her lap.........
Her coat of arms, a dingy, worn out, card board sign
"Please help, I'm homeless, with my infant child!"
Blind mankind walking past
Let them die, wild animals need to eat
Animals over humans

Tripping Balls

It's called Rome once again
We stumble in this world like blind rats
Scurrying to go nowhere fast
Our destination, unknown
Except in the ground
Then will we learn
While a creator asks
"What was done?"
Excuses will fill the streets
Lost in a world full of hopes
Full of dreams
Big shots in the city of make believe
Sickness fills the world
An existence gone corrupt
"What's the disease?"
Some PHD of common sense gives the prognosis
A plague, labeled greed
Printed green
Enough, to give everyone what they need
Though, no one has enough to make ends meet
In a city of make believe
A bench with two
On the street called dreams
No home to call their own
Lost in the madness of it all
Begging like dogs, though dogs
Have better treatment after all
Remember this is the streets
Where humanity lost its feet
The crows feast upon the eyes
No wonder humanity can't see
A small child with wide brown eyes
Looks about, wearing clothing so dirty
So, worn, not even the corporation of Goodwill wants them

Shunned at the door called civilized
It's all about money
Just another soul, fallen
Into the cracks of society
Too focused on mindless entertainment
A small child with wide brown eyes
Standing by a man
Who hasn't had a shower in days, weeks, months
Just reeks
Digging through a trash can
An attempt, find something to eat
Pain runs deep
It's written upon their countenance
DEPRESSION, a melody
Performed by the band Utter Defeat
World walks on
Its eyes, heavenly focused
Some artificial fictional prize
All in the city of make believe
The plaque upon the head
"What's in it for me?"
Too busy, chasing imagination
Blessings at the feet
Organisms, left begging in streets
Except these are human beings
Society too fucked up
Down trodden with CIA drugs
America, bring in the police
A new regime
Beating down the already broken
They only ask what's in it for me
In a city of make believe

Tripping Balls

C

```
Let's have a police state
Treat it like a video game
Bust out the champagne
     we got something to celebrate
```

Walking into Oblivion

I've come into the world
Like a crashing star
Not recognized by anyone
Set galaxies apart
An alien among the norm
Not one grasps me
Not even my kin
Looking for home
In the goddamn abyss
Walking into oblivion
Lost in the future
Not living for the day
Chasing tomorrow
With broken wings
These eyes tell a story
Born to be societies cheap rag
Shoving pins in my eyes
Helps me numb the pain
Thy only light
Smiling in worst of times
I'm broken down
No love in sight
Seeking, been seeking
So, goddamn long
For love above all else
My arms stretched wide
Feeling like I'm ripped apart
Given till I bleed
Returned not to me
Now just a closed door
A pile of rubble

Tripping Balls

Fairy tales of a heart beat
Walking into oblivion
Lost in the future
Not living for the day
Chasing tomorrow
With broken wings
These eyes tell a story
Born to be societies cheap rag doll
Shoving pins in my eyes
Help me numb the pain
Thy only light
Smiling in worst of times
I'm broken down
No love in sight
Here to not be seen
Just want you to notice me
Pounding as you walk past me
Stuck in this glass
Your eyes cold, so cold
Ignored the expectation, so cold
This heart......shattered
All that remained, lost to the grave
Walking into oblivion
Lost in the future
Not living for the day
Chasing tomorrow
With broken wings
These eyes tell a story
Born to be societies
cheap rag doll
Shoving pins in my eyes
Help me numb the pain
Thy only light

Smiling in worst of times

Gocni Schindler

I'm broken down
No love in sight
Give me hope
Just something
Touch me, let me feel
Wanting you to love me
Show me, let me see
Been requesting so damn long
Let me believe, believe that
I'm more than nothing
Put me back together
Just one reason
Walking into oblivion
Lost in the future
Not living for the day
Chasing tomorrow
With broken wings
Just give me a reason
To breathe!

I WON THE LOTTO

I made national news!
The reporter asking
Probing me for answers......
Worthless questions in scope of reality
"What will you do with all the money?"
I thought for a moment, then retorted
Perhaps at first
I'll buy a politician, always wanted a parasite for a pet.
Least this way they will actually work
for the people, not some foreign banker's needs
Best not say that too loud though, don't want to be
harassed by their IRS.
I don't know, maybe I'll bribe a main stream media reporter
to actually report on real news.
You know, actually do their job! Unbiasedly, like real journalists do.
Maybe, I'll give some to a church, who will
not buy themselves some television equipment, or fancy
$4000.00 suits or a new BMW to parade it around in front of
the people they are supposed to serve.
No, a church that will
actually do the work of their alleged Lord
who they say they serve.
Use the money, helping to get the homeless off the curb.
Perhaps, I'll create another media social outlet, only this
one won't be secretly controlled by the government
while being run by a nut job.
Maybe
I'll take it all, pile it in front of this unconstitutional
Federal Reserve and burn it!
Sending a message, that us humans are not to be owned.

Maybe I'll attempt to make an antigravity ship,
Fly up into space and bitch slap E.T in that thing called a face.
With this much toilet paper,
the possibilities are quite endless.

Living on Empty

Living on empty
No white picket fences
Given to music, a lonely joy
No early morning surprise
An oasis is my soul
Singing is my living
Living kinda small
No one ever hears me
Cover band not this show
Originality has no place
Where corporations rest their flags
Once a land of opportunity
Mindlessness runs the course

Living on empty
No white picket fences
Given to music, a lonely joy
No early morning surprise
An oasis is my soul
Living while existing
Life was riding me
Breaking this body
Broken down
Survivals new toy
Comfort makes me fearful
Locked away in a cage
Never taking chances
Anything like wishing upon the sea
Dreams, broken words
Crosses lips.

Living on empty
No white picket fences

Gocni Schindler

Given to music, a lonely joy
No early morning surprise
An oasis is my soul
Love of my life
Music, that soulful joy
Real in thy heart
Bleeding an old Irish song
Blue print of life
Insanely broken down
Lost in an empty hole
Begging for rope
Don't hear my plea
Living on empty
No white picket fences
Given to music, that lonely joy
No early morning surprise
An oasis is my soul
An oasis the one place I call my own.

Dear Zombies

Did you lose your device?
DISSIDENCE gave a call
No response
OUTRAGE commented on your status
Lost in the maze
REASON tweeted a shout
Ignored just the same
LOGIC sent an Instagram
Never gazed
JUSTICE sent an email
Must have been spammed
IGNORANCE sent a text
The convo never ends

Gocni Schindler

LOST IT ALL

A head rings loud, rings clear
Seeking so hard, so long
For this illustrious dream
Love hitting out of the right-side clear
knocking all plans laid on the table of life clear
Crashing down to the dirty floor
It was all there
Who you are
What you stood for
Just real genuine true!
Was always rugged
Always so cold, forced tough
Born to be alone
It was just for I, In life
Until you came crashing through my walls
Like some champion lion that knew your place
You shined so bright like the morning light
All darkness, chased away
You exposed my very being
The fear gripped me
The world seen through me
Your eyes, so deep, sincere
Seen in me
The depths of my pain you embraced
Knew so well in yourself
Love over powered my mental state
With a simple touch, instant sanity
So many, many, many have I met
None to ever look only noticing a human shell
So lost would I get in your world
Your arms found me safe, found me secure
My fear prevailed in this event
Thoughts prevail all your love

Tripping Balls

I'm going crazy with crazy
My eyes look to space
You're nowhere to be found
I'm a train wreck, just another lost event
Driving you away like jumping off a cliff
Those words echo in my mind
Give me your heart, it's all you desired.
Seeking your warmth
Lonely yet cold
What remains
please come back to me
Longing for that safe place
Resting my head upon
Your bare skin
These weak fingers
Finding peace in your strength
All this safety is now gone
Like a floating memory
Fades away.
Going crazy in this brain
Your love made me complete
In the dark of night
I cry so hard to have you
Nowhere do I belong
Everywhere have I been
Why did I push so hard?
Fear gripped me
Giving me voids
If found completion inside
Now nothing remains
I drove you away
come back was the plea
Longing for that safe place
Resting my head upon
Your bare skin chest

These weak fingers
Finding peace in your hands
All this safety is now gone
like a floating memory that
Fades away
You loved me so deep
Believed in me, made me safe
Threw it away
Just a scared little girl
Seeking some place
So, lost without you
This soul aches
Wanting that touch
Energy filled the room
Fireworks ignite
Our souls combined
You were my safety
My lifelong love
What I destroyed
Please come back
Longing for that safe place
Resting my head upon
Your bare skin chest
These weak fingers
Finding peace in your hands
All this safety is now gone
A floating memory that
Fades away fades away
Praying so hard to find a way
That would have your free spirit back with me
Feel the pain of emptiness
Feel what love was
Giving the world to have you back
The price would never be enough
Every wall I ever had is nothing but piles now

Tripping Balls

Insides exposed, it was me that drove you away
Baby, please come back
Longing for that safe place
Resting my head upon bare skin chest
These weak fingers finding peace in your hands
I've lost you, I have no peace in my land

WHAT IF

Let's ask this?
If Jesus and Mohammed were gay lovers
Who would be the man?
Who would be the bitch?
Isn't that a thought!
Hope you didn't just wet your pants with hate
Wanting to burn the world down
Because of some words
That really didn't mean anything
All for a religion, provided by man.

EVIL

It gave me hope, then you spoke
Discovering I'd never be
Anything to you
Wanted, only when it was fitting
Dig open, those wounds
Walk through wearing high heels.
Burn me with rays
Eyes held so dear
Like looking into paradise
Burning, burnt to a crisp
Heart black like coal
Blackness
Leading me down the road
Losing my soul
Your only care, your own
Bring it up, bring it to me again
I really want to know
Tell me your hurt
Tell me, oh please, please enlighten me
On how awful it felt
Boldly compare it, refer to my own
Voice screams deceit
Reason states we walked this before
Evil, evilest acts of bad
A well-known friend
Those voices scream to me
Imaginations flourish all the more
Soul sinking low
Bottom so well known
Darkness my only friend
It wasn't 'til I fell wholly in love with a woman
That I discovered just how wicked this world really is
Don't ever give your heart wholly to a woman,

Gocni Schindler

They'll only destroy it
Without care about anything except self.
Your message like a light in darkness
I loved wholly, never make the mistake again

ADVERTISEMENT

Brand Y brings to you another great line of products
Please take a hand full of our delicious GMO's.
Chase it down with this fruity Fluoride.
Our products are 100% natural!
We have a stamp from the FDA.
Yes, that means, it's perfectly safe

WEEK OLD CHICKEN DINNER

Meet Jim
He's a beautiful soul
For Jim, it's just another day in America
Living under the street bridge
In a cardboard mansion
At least the rain stays away
In a tent, he bartered for some trash
Having nowhere to call home
Cops show up telling him to go
Jim used to have a job
Allowing him to just scrape by
He wasn't smart enough
In the NEW EDUCATIONAL SOCIETY
He's from a time
When working with your hands was a way to survive
Then someone, a bankster superstar came along
With more money than god
Wanted to make extraordinary profits
The GOV with lust infested eyes
Wanted to help this BANKER ROCKSTAR along
Let's endorse
Let's support
Let's start promoting cheap labor
In another state?
Hell NO!!
But rather, a different part of the world
Apart of the "Bigger, better, more" Laws
Where good ethics
Just got tossed out the door
So now, Jim has nothing
No skills for the new future
In the land of American pie
Sing us another song

Tripping Balls

Politician sluts
Just another used car sales rep
Pitching an end of the year sales event
Cause we believe in all this shit
Great change, isn't that right Jim?
How's it under the bridge
It surely is safe at night, isn't it?
The Politician made a promise
That was for one class of people
The Rich as he shouted Middle class
No one asked
What about the no CLASS?
Oh, life of pleasures living under a bridge
Dream up another classic speech
That your writers will write oh, politician
Though for people like Jim
It's hard to dream
When the food you eat
Week old chicken dinner
That ya just found in a trash can
Sure, is great isn't it, Jim?

Gocni Schindler

Bankers give it to you dry

THE ACT

A magician waves his hand.
The dove appears.
The media waves its hand.
The truth disappears.
Two great illusionists.
One makes things appear
The other makes them disappear.
One harmless entertainment
The other a lying whore!

Gocni Schindler

**Journalism dinner is dead.
Propaganda, now served at Six!
Want Fries with that?**

THE GREAT ILLUSION

It all starts somewhere
From the beginning
Something to be better
Someone to be less
Get killed over
Lack of self
Finding worth in falsity
In an instance
Wealth is more sacred
More respected
Accumulate
What's expected
It's all just to be washed away
The great illusion
Filling the emptiness
For mere moments
Only to be back
With more emptiness
Same created reality
Nothingness
Seeing not what is real
Cruelty of life
Fleshly eyes
So, limited
Hands that feel
What isn't real
The things in this realm
A great illusion
Paying till death

Gocni Schindler

Behold; I seen a white flag!
Citizens, knew not what it
meant. Great calamity was heard,
like a voice upon the wind
Anger shook the ground;
injustice, what was said!

Tripping Balls

Welcome to the World

Sometimes, in this schizoid of a world
A soul goes to the point of destruction
Having no way back to what was before
It was forced to shut down
REBOOTING System Errors, Complete refresh
Not functioning to the fullest
Thoughts race
Destroyed what was innocent
It's one big mess
Finding new purpose
Nothing makes sense
It's all just a riddle
Trying to escape
Can't escape from self
It's a disaster
Answers so few
Hardly to be found
The voices are of no help
Called from an abyss of darkness
It doesn't make sense
The last ten years
Blurred
Feeling like a wondering fool
Not knowing where to go
Patience lost in this madness
Wanting a fresh release
Opened this mind
Things got crazy
Too much understanding
Nine to five
Boring melancholy
An intended purpose
This is purposely developed madness

Solely for the lust of greed
Made in any place far from home
Thieves took your jobs
Making you beg
Another money slave
Children to be raised
Reality just make believe
Brainwashed by a system
To only enslave
Subservient to their will
Starvation the only bet
Open thine eyes
Before thou wilt die

What IF
**THIS IS ALL JUST A FICKLE
ILLUSION, LIFE HAS NO MEANING,
SO DON'T YOU WORRY, NOT ONE BIT,
NOTHING IS REAL, WHEN YOU LIVE
IN THE SHIT!**

Complacency, Your Dead End

It's a system that's broken
A game that's all wrong.
Just continue to play along
While living another rerun
Complacency, crotch drippings dream
Humanity, nothing more than a group of frogs
Tossed into a pan of water, set to the fire
Soon all will be dead
Some Alien entity will take over
Stupid humanity
Gave away your home
Your rights
For the Government's loving arms
IF the citizen dies it's alright!
If the agent of the government dies;
Well then, someone needs to be held ACCOUNTABLE.
Someone will take the fall!
No matter if they're guilty of the act at all!
They...........must..............pay!
The government, higher in value
than the citizen it was meant to serve.

Tripping Balls

RAPED NATIVE FOLK

In the mass of prejudice
Held strong by the dead hand of justice
Persecuted was the people
Harassed, starved
Driven from what was theirs
Thieves that brought a god
Liars, that took what they didn't earn
A group of people
Chippewa, what they called'em
Shoved into the corner of the world
Savages, was a label they worn proud
Living off the land, a glorious crown
GLORIOUS TO THOSE WHO ARE SHUNNED!
Tossed to the ground
Their women, their children
Left to starve, it's for the cross
Trampled 'til destroyed
Make no mention, let it be forgot
In the world of civilized
Momma cried when the FBI died
This place torn apart
Fiction of make believe
Agents in a land
Coming to a place, they didn't belong
Looking for an eagle, with worn out boots
'CAUSE THAT BULLSHIT IS BELIEVABLE!
A group of brothers
Bounded, by the times of persecution
Bound by loyalty and love
Sick of the prejudice
Cancer upon a raped land
No one to know, who took the first shot
It's the government

Gocni Schindler

They do what they want
Time to make an excuse
One man to take a fall
Crucify this person
He's NOT HUMAN!
Make an example
Create lies
Document them
File them away
Abraham to hang the savages
No one, will ever know the truth anyway
GOVERNMENT NEVER LIES!
Harass a woman to tell a fable
A well written script
Threaten
Aggressive force
It's in your power
Rights you have
You've taken inches
Now it's up in feet
JUSTICE they called it
If the price is right
Away with it
Put that filth Native in a cage
Though, you should have known
Wrong doings own the voice
Eyes aren't always blind
Truth trumps deceit
Eagle lost its wings
THE FBI GOT REVENGE
The innocent rots in a cage
Free Leonard Peltier

Unilluminated

Drop a nuke already
Get the show on the road
I got me a lawn chair
A case of suds
Going to sit down and relax
In front of the entrance to your hidden campground
You think all of us will die
Funny thing
You'll never make it inside

Diary of the Non-Influential Man

It's the 13th day on an undisclosed month
Entering this world at 1:20 PM
My name would come soon enough
As the parent laid eyes upon me
I was probably kicking, most assuredly screaming
I had no idea of what was to come
This is day one
To what would lead to a series of events
Outta my control
For as we are born into this world
We are but for a short time
Corrupted, through our environment
With time, we are produced into what we will become
For the cards dealt to us
Most hold close, except of course
For those that break the mold
Your ass is free
Sign here:
_____

Run wild, be young, don't live for tomorrow
LIVE TO BE

HUMANITY O'HUMANITY

This shit box
No more like
Round shit-hole
That's better
Some give it title
Mother Earth
It's a lady 'cause it gives birth
Gotta wonder, who brings the CUM
Villains that live upon it
Birthed, destroying everything
Killing Mommy, what fun?
Let's start
Getting carried away with nonsense
Entertainment rules the show
Give the rats some pretty lights
While injecting them with shots of strychnine
Reality is what one is lead to believe
Fool the mind
It's easily obtained
beings who rarely think
Drinking away common sense
Piss it down a drain
Drink some more
Pharma your life away
INSECTS
Gladly take your spot
Let your guard dog
Run wild
Shitting in neighbor's yards
Someone eventually
Needs to pay
Barbarism
Mindless savages

In modern clothing
Full of wealth
Eating flesh
Thinking themselves
A higher life
Nothing more than anyone
Subject to death
Replicated, just a copy, of something else
We create what we are
Creations that break
That come to an end
A computer program
With its glitches
Humans, nothing more
Nothing less
All of us replicated
From something else
Just a program
Learned to repeat
Steps from our past
A bigger brain
More intelligence
In the last 50 years
Magic waved its hand
Give an illusion
Set it as reality
You lost your land
Set to cost
You lost your health
Set to cost
Want it back?
Give'em
The debt notes
Investors
Anyone can have a debt

Tripping Balls

Masters
Hold the trump cards
Their Royal Flush
Pummeling that full house
Suckers that still lost
Get hungry
Be depressed
Excuses for
Eating shit
Not fit for animals
Nor insects
It's all part of the plan
Trust your life
To a GOVERNMENT
They know
What is BEST
Corporate puppets
Running the FDA
Lost your damn mind
Robbed your ass
Did it with a sales pitch
SUCKERS
Fool, would be better
Though, that would mean
Lack of choice
Civilization
One to rule
Civilization
One to destroy
Civilization
Make weapons
Be it a rock
Be it a gun
Media spins propaganda
Human Kind

Kind, use to be part of the word
'Til it got tossed
Into that corporate waste
It just wasn't
Politically correct
Dirt beneath feet
Be the animal
Locked away in a cage
Not in a prison
Reverted to being nothing
Lower than dirt
INSECTS
Gladly taking that place
After the feast
Cleaning up the mess
Achieving the stars
Foot tripped on the rock
Crashing to the ground
Wake up, wake up
What you think you have
Really has you
We are all slaves
Even those who think
They're exposing some mystical truth

Tripping Balls

TEN to ONE

Childish fun
TEN triumphant kings
Ruled a vast land
NINE years of war
Fighting for a hand
EIGHT Noble Kings
Remained to kill the day
SEVEN maiden's chosen
To bring peace
SIX maidens had boys
All at the same time
FIVE days late
She was born
FOUR kings gathered
Scheming against FOUR
THREE planned the end
Truly one stood back
TWO did the deed
Now the few at hand
ONE would finish the two
Taking the Land
ONE obtained above all else
Ruling self with loneliness
TWO Noble men felt bad
Approached with a plan
THREE ideas to save the day
Presented to one maddening king
FOUR small minutes; sheer chaos
Wonderful, glamorous outrages
FIVE miniscule guards
Toss dead noblemen to the curb
SIX empty wine bottles; drank in the day
Kicked; busted by a wall of shame

SEVEN lucky servants
Cleaning it singing Hooray
EIGHT dogs sent running
King in a maddening haze
NINE minks in the corner
Hands folded to pray
TEN Beautiful lights
Filling the night
TEN tears fall
King has it all.
NINE Fingers feel a face
Skin worn thin
EIGHT years plus a few blue moons
Something to brew
SEVEN birds a jerkin
The message coming soon
SIX grown boys
Now young men
FIVE seeking vengeance
Justice upon their heads
FOUR swords sharpening
Bring rest to the day
THREE days to quell the brood
Old King more ruthless
TWO grown boys now men
Stand trial, malcontent
ONE last hope in the distance
Riding on a majestic steed
ONE caramel colored horse
Called "SUCCESS"
TWO steps to the side
Never behind
THREE steps ahead
Conquering was the path
FOUR devastating lots

Tripping Balls

Now was the time
FIVE Risked it all
Just another shot
SIX little Beauties
Lacking beauty as hers
SEVEN minks in a fountain
Stunned by a goddess on earth
EIGHT Breathtaking Blue swans
Guide her very feet
NINE Powerful aromas upon her skin
Putting even the Nobleman to a knee
TEN elegant flasks
Elegance only in her hands
TEN to bring peace
Eternal in sleep
NINE Glasses taken out
Servants set them up
EIGHT did she fill
Left one empty she did
SEVEN drinks; guards one each
The KING receives two
SIX dancing beauties
Purposely distracting
FIVE servants delivering
Two young men; not so beloved
FOUR swallows; one glass 'til it's gone
The whole nine of them fall
THREE white spheres
Picking souls
TWO float towards heaven
Playing harpsichords
ONE
For thy admiration, of course

BLACK HAIR

Hair, lots of it
Thick, long, black hair
Thick, like a cotton mop
Wet with sweat
Across the pillow top
Wrapped around that neck
Blown in the wind
Eyes, lifeless
Look down the side
Given like a gift
Draping over a dress
In the moment
Horrific death
Sexy, isn't it?

Green Rain

I saw a UFO
E.T. was flying it.
Stopping over me
it opened a door.
Light peered out
badly hurting my eyes.
It was damn blinding, you know.
"Jesus", I cried!
Then it started raining.
It was the stench of death
wrapped in wet
The door closed
like seconds flat.
The UFO was gone from sight
It also stopped raining!
Damn, was so cool
seeing a UFO.
Just don't know
What all the green shit is

Gocni Schindler

Ted Rice, Was it all just a dream?

Meet Dick and Jane

They don't do shit
Ten cars in the garage
It's what they need to live
Richer than the richest
Their kids have no worries
Just built them a two hundred thousand dollar
house in a tree. Life sure is rough for them
The only issue they have is who they can trust
Dick made a wise decision a few years back
Took daddy's company to another market.
Goods that use to be made in America
Now made overseas for next to nothing.
Though, the prices never dropped
In good old US of A.
Coincidentally though
Quality did, that hit the floor!
Dick and Jane didn't care, just run it into the ground
All about the profits these days
PROFITS that they will never be able to spend!
America, sure is great, isn't it?
Dick and Jane

THE TALE

It was a cold night
Sweatshirt type weather
Oops, a hoodie
An unexpected meeting
Accidentally sitting
Near one another
Fleshly arousal
Tingles upon the skin
Hair that stood on end
Though eyes
Never made contact
Spiritual eyes did
Familiar spirits
Well known to one another
Though, never known at all
The energy embrace
Would not be broken
'Til the time
Had expired
The journey
Would be hard to over come
Though that imitation love
Like wild growing flowers
Don't be fooled, just weeds
Exploding from the ground
Beholding the imitation bloom
This rhetoric is from
An imitation romance novel
The voice of beauty; all but silenced
A cockroach, sits in the corner
The Contemplator Contemplating, leads to madness
Well, so they say
Hope, creates another day

Tripping Balls

Long as the moon decides to stay
The minds focus on time, not given
Body regrets, time, that has passed
All but walk on a spinning ball
Leading, to the same destination
Ignorance, destroys what intelligence brings
Human value
Less than a dog, these days
Give an overabundance
Approbation on the great difference
between a civilized barbarian
Or that of a savage
Only showing
That one can speak
While the other, just mumbles
Tongues, best served to be removed
Yet the two of them
Still can't think
Portion of the world
Expects a monkey in a space ship
To save them
While another section
Expects some, drunken river boat captain
To lead them
Few understand
They rule their own universe....
Answers quickly to a bold tongue
A powerful mind
Only for the contemplator
Who is bum shit crazy
Of course
Labeled, by the brilliant ones in society
The two classes of barbarians
Fight for an argument
The monkey in the spaceship

holding a banana in one hand
A golf club in the other
Races across a moonlit sky
Off, to another fund raiser
Meanwhile
A riverboat captain
Pours another one of his famous Rum N Cokes
The Contemplator contemplating
Stops to ask......
"What is the reason for an argument other than to enforce
what opinion should be followed and the attitude of I rule?"
The crowd looks in dumbness
So, the Contemplator asks again
"What did one really rule but a simple idea?"
The drunken river boat captain
That everyone seems to want
Finishes his 15th Jack N Coke
Scratching his ass
Gets the great idea
He is ready to lead the ranks
But first
He needs to get his drunk ass
On the deck of the boat
The result of the mindless
That lets him think
Yet again
Makes another, irrational mistake
Taking it upon himself
Making the contemplator, walk the plank
Meanwhile
The river washes away such futility
Floating, face down
Only purpose

Tripping Balls

Feeding fish
Tear away at flesh
Exposing bone
Soon will rest
Where not even angels tread
The Contemplator
Must have been insane
All but lost
Thoughts leading to much distress
According to the drunken
Wisdom inspired
River boat captain
Thinking, too much of a dangerous task
Then one day, the moon realizes
He's not even getting paid for what he does
People, on the ball that spins
so, ungrateful
He just says
"Fuck this!"
All the while
Barbarians fight
Over who won the argument
The cockroach looks up then states
"What a chaotic mess this is gonna be!"
In the crazy event that follows
Civilized barbarians just wet themselves
Look at the monkey in the sky
Flying a spaceship
The MONKEY
Making some chimp noises that translate
"Fuck me, I can't land this pile!"
Then The captain of the vessel
Who was so quick
To toss the contemplator to the sea
Sitting in the corner sucking his thumb

While a billion, pissed off non-talking barbarians
stand over him with clubs
The voice of The Contemplator
That had the balls to ask
Now all but bones
Laying on the bottom, of some shit infested sea bed
Where not even angels tread
All the fully-wise river boat captain can say
as his brains are getting bashed
"Bullets would feel better than clubs!"
The Monkey, flying the spaceship
CRASHES into Mt. Everest
Civilized barbarians, are all but wrecked
Meanwhile, the cockroach
That no one seemed to notice
Is doing his song and dance
For in the end; he's the only one left

Tripping Balls

For a quick prank, I made a bumper sticker. It stated Fuck the Pope. I placed it on the rear of the Holy Priest's car. Then had the pleasure of watching him drive around town. A few that laughed with me. He couldn't decipher why all the stares, why all the laughter. Mrs. Goody helped him remove it. What beasts could do such things? Always someone to ruin the fun. These are just humans playing gods. None have the answers, no, not one!
It's not impossible to climb out of the abyss

PRISON

The metal; on wrist, on ankle
Cold to the skin
Hard steel rubs against flesh
Fittingly matching a broken soul
If one wanted to know
Eyes from the judge
Gray like a cold winter
Blazoned with earnest sincerity
His face doesn't give a shit
About who you are
Where you came from
The sentence handed down
As stated
Bad hand at cards, no damn excuse
A new born felon
Excellent badge of shame
Life changing, face the doom
Acceptance hits like a freight train
Bring to life no excuse
Be it, broken down
From that side of town
Walking away
Lead back to a cage
The metal off wrists
METAL
Removed from ankles
Small amounts of light
Trickles in
Though everything
Dark
Blackened, my world inside
Fear destroys all
Tears roll in, laughter prevails

Tripping Balls

Moment arrives to the door
Into the transport
It's a long haul
ARRIVAL
GATES TO HELL
Gladiator school
Open wide to a brown box
Out of the transport
Stripped down
Nakedness in other's eyes shaming
Sitting in a room, thirty other ruthless apes
SHAMED, disgraced
Given white powder
Chemical bath
Injected with shots
No longer human, fucking lab rats
Birth to something different
Animal instincts in madness
Only strong survive, fighting for nothing
Nothing is everything
Two socks, a lock, weapon of choice
Kindness, mercy
That Sunday school preaching
Flushed down the drain
Turn another cheek
That shit is for the weak
Every day A New terror
Mind your own
Keep silent, speak nothing
Borrow nothing from the store
Owe no one
Follow simple rules
CONFRONTATION
Never back down
Not once, not ever

In the home of the vile
Blackness wears the crown
Luciferin ideas
Do as thou wilt
There is no honor
Lifeless worth.... Life
Not worth two packs of smokes
In a cage
Murderers, Rapists, Thieves
Worst of the vile in hell
Kingdom for the illusion
HUMANITY
The bunk-box
All full of your shit
Only possessions
Shit, worth nothing to an outside world
All but robbed
Voices sound off
What's been done
Two socks, one lock
JUSTICE
It's just dogs
Urinating on their ground
Brought hard, monsters
No boundaries, pain beloved
Destroying man
White Shirts just fat fuck's
Not smart enough to be cops
Take one down, two if you're good
Six rip you to shreds
Stripped to nakedness
Tossed in the box
The door slams shut
Darkness, new best friend
Thirty days slow like a bad dream

Tripping Balls

The light burns
Rage finds a home
Wanting to kill this system
For this inhumanity
Nothing is nothing
Survive, no meaning
Dangerous ground
Create the killer
Never meant to be free to begin with
Still over shit materials
Man, never learns in the corner
Six on one
Pay no mind, not your fight
Never the aggressor...
Gangs rule that show
They'll fall faster to the ground
The Natural rule
Swallow some balloons
Prison drugs
Shit them out
Hell's palace
Called entrapment
Over a year into this
SHIT, nine more to go
Life hasn't even begun
Death, every where
Shanking's, blood spills
Like broken faucets, shit spews all over the floor
Nothing Precious, NOTHING
Fools call it respect
HONOR with the dogs
EVIL has none
It's for love of violence
Part of the boy's game
In the lowest part of fictional humanity

Parole board meeting
Excited for a chance
Shot down
Lesson learned, no hope for tomorrow
Life has no meaning, fuck them
You're your own keeper
Hands to rip, to tear
Fragile Human beings
Survival of another day
Societies plan
Never letting you out
Pieces of you gone
DAMAGED goods
Beyond repair
The former no more
Easily catch another case
It's game over
Lifetime in the cage
Society, too far from reach
Numbness as time disappears
Have no contact
Momma, your son is no more
Her tears; weakness ya can't have
Hold no importance
The outside world
Gone for good
Make life easier
It's what needs to be told
These self-lips only truth
Insanity steps in
Soon, nothing even to give a shit
Follow the rules
That keep you breathing
Life passes away
Locked in a cage

Tripping Balls

Another parole board meeting
Look at these fictional stooges
Sitting behind that table
Like their gods
Phonies, fakes, dead
The mouth utters without thinking
Quit wasting my damn time
That game of spades
Of more importance
Yes, you learned a lesson
Life is a work of fiction
I'm in a cage
You got the monster
Shame me
Violate my humanity
Beat me, rectal exam me
Sadist faggots in closets march
Destroy what's left
Act like Gods in here
Beings without souls
Live like an animal
Suddenly; supposed to care
Back to the cage
Just leave the room
Throw me back in a hole
Darkness loves me
I need the sleep
Time passes
Forward it goes
Hair grayish
Still in youth
Time, soon to be released
To hell with Parole
Felon, a badge of shame
Surviving a societal hell

Gocni Schindler

It's now a pride thing

Actor Man

It's an odd life
Full ups and downs
Minimal gains
Set backs
Being one paycheck from homelessness
One day, it's a special type of day
Actor Man whose name is yet
Well shit, that's another mystery
Actor Man was on the path
Titled down loser's road
Almost to live under a bridge
Living from place to place
Another room to rent
Another, year in the books
Getting ancient in the land
Some fucking Botox, Nips, then Tucks
Maintain a flakiness
Its Red Carpets
Photographs with the pretenders
Ass kissing events
Getting one to nowhere land
More bullshit photos with no ones
After the shower
Before the next audition
That mug in the mirror
Give that look
Pretend it's before
Millions of people
A STAR
Make more in porn
Six points if a Jew
They own the town
Least that is what Actor Man said

You're getting an academy award
Oh, how you love them
Don't ya?
Great self-speeches
GREAT INDEED
Motivational uplifts
Read from pages
Ripped from the daily Calendar
One of those
Ya hocked from the free clinic
Tell yourself
"You're the greatest!"
Pop another one of those
Prozac's 80mg, Percocet's 325
Over the hill, down the throat
Like your momma done when you were born
Soon the medicine
Makes the world numb
Off to the big audition
This is the one
Actor Man feels it
Thousands on social media
Never are they fucking wrong
Not ever, they know it all
Open a door, stroll down the hall
The ROOM
A room full of stooges and Barbie's
On the path to fame, riches
Five minutes of look-at-me assholes
Aren't you jealous now?
It's a great audition
So, they say, hell they always say
Just... not... good... enough!
DAMN, must be too tall
(Laugh of the day)

Tripping Balls

Not getting that part
Actor Man, just not what they're looking for
Days upon days of analyzing
Terrorizing all those stumbling around
With depressing talks
 "Why didn't I get that part?"
Drama king, it's 'cause you suck!
Actor Man sure isn't waving that
MAGICAL HOLLYWOOD WAND
Must have been too tall
No, No, that isn't it
Way too short
Too fat, too thin, so frustrating...isn't it?
Not muscular enough
Hit the gym, fool
So many superficial things
Forget about the acting part
That has nothing to do with it
Magic is in if they like you
Try treating them like humans
The next audition
The same shit yet again
Must be stuck on repeat
The car ride home
In that pile of AIDS
Registered in another state
Poor dreamers can't afford
To register their cars
In the land of make believe
Los Angeles, USA!
Back to a bedroom
Another actor rented room
Back to a drawing board
Park the car on the street
Two miles from the rented room

The damn car in a Nazi-Ville
Have to move it in four hours
Avoid those pesky tickets for fame
Damn those parking officer pricks
They'll steal your car
You gotta pay, fuck-a-stain
Onto the infamous walk
Mind doesn't quit
It's Why, Why, Why to the front door
The key
Shit where did Actor Man put the key?
In one of a dozen pockets
Actors are eccentric, didn't ya know?
The key, it's hallelujah
Hand slides key into the door knob
Like religion, it's all about sex
Unlock that gated style door
The door opens
Actor Man's eyes wide open now
A wondrous awful sight
Room Lord buck-ass naked
In plain sight
Just standing there
Cock blows in the wind
If there was wind to blow
Bigger than a sail mast
Dude, put Anaconda away
No shame, says Actor Man's brain
Room Lord's attitude
It's who gives a fuck!
I live in L.A. land of make believe
He's eating a sandwich
Don't like it in magicland, get out
Just another bullshit day
As he smiles

Tripping Balls

"How did the audition go?"
Actor Man can't believe what is taking place
It's just another bump in the road
The Room Lord
FROWNS
"Cat got your tongue, wonder boy?"
Actor Man still speechless, struggles to muster a sound
"Did alright, I guess, it could have gone better!"
Always the same lame excuse
The Room Lord places the sandwich to his mouth
Some mustard drips over a hairy, naked chest
Actor Man disgusted
The Room Lord just looks at Actor Man
"You're Fucking Weird, Actor Boy, maybe you should try
Porn, it pays more, besides, not like you have a soul!"
The Room Lord walks away shaking his ass
Leaving off some healthy farts!
All in a day's life of Actor Man!
Off to another audition
Off to another person's couch
Its life!
Give that self-speech
You're going to MAKE IT
Another chasing vanity
On the path to fame
Should have done porn
It pays more

Gocni Schindler

Red Carpet Events
Simply the best

SAVE THE DAY

As time progresses
Things seem to get worse
One wants to sit in the house to hide
Life via the tele
The world made of people
The same species
Fooled into believing in races
Two wants to fix things, though age
Not in favor
Lost without a map
Give them a Beeline
Three wants to understand the past
Looking back to see ahead
Four, looking upon the paths to the future
Stepping to another direction
Five to find the courage
Always digging a hole
Six, a mental case
Lost that mind along the way
Seven, the brave
A non-conformist
Eight, the mindless mighty
Not smart enough to know anything but brutality
Nine lost to the scene, yet, making a come back

Some have labeled this vessel of flesh as a practitioner of existentialism. Never was one who followed labels. Don't really give a damn! Finding critiquing life annoying, purest futility.

BAD DAY

It's just one of those days
It's this cesspool airport
Mouse-town Orlando
Might as well be called hell
Filled with kids, little piss n shits
Runny noses, fucking coughing
Spreading filth and germs
All for some magic kingdom
Some stupid fucking mouse
Just another ten grand
Dumped in the toilet
It's easy, like taking a healthy shit
Two overweight old fucks
Probably came to this toilet for golf
Disgust fills their fat faces
Looking like they gotta squeeze one off
Somewhere, amazingly
Someone loves these pricks
Sure, isn't anyone in here
To hell with getting old
Smoke, drink, then smoke some more
Suddenly people want to live to be 100 years old
Have fun drooling on yourself
Next, we have some cum stain
wearing some Cal Lutheran hoodie
Talking to his overweight chic friend
About her logical death
"Skin Cancer!"
Most likely, he says
Like he has any damn clue
He sits like a queen
Crosses those legs like a broad
Trying to keep its vagina closed

Gocni Schindler

I would have respect if he adorned a dress
This damn white family of five
Five little scrappers
Kids that can't sit still
Bouncing all over the damn place
I'm bitching like I'm ninety-one and a half
Oh great, look at that
The little girl
"Princess"
Just dumped the contents
Of her momma's purse
There it goes
All over the floor
Isn't that cute?
Awe, such a little angel
More like a demon in pink
I thought only Mexicans had this many kids
The good catholic ones, that is!
The mom, despicably over-weight
Just sits there looking dumb
With a sandwich in her hand
Her mate picks up the shit from her bag
Nice tampon-white mother of five
Why don't ya have another?
Make it an even six
That cotton wad for your crotch
Would have saved the Titanic on April 15th
Yeah, that's it, take another big bite
I'd love to shove that sandwich down your throat
While peering down at your mate
Telling the ball-less bastard, this is how it's done
oh, did you find your nut sack in that bag of hell?
It doesn't matter
The guy still gives you the dick
You're already overweight

Tripping Balls

"GROSS"
Fuck, get me out of this hell
Two Orientals
Wanting to be called Asians
I think they're a couple
Their eyes fixated
Glued to their smart devices
Cables coming out of their heads
Like mini black-haired cyborgs
I bet they don't even speak
Not sure they know what lips are for
Let alone the tongue
Can't wait to get the hell out of this place
This mouse trap area from the pit of hell
Fuck this tourist bullocks
Time to get back to L.A.
Get away
From these rodents called KIDS!

END

It's suddenly a dire threat.
One bar filled with people
Why not go out with style
In the end
Drinks and more drinks
Jimmy
That was his name
He was tallish with flowing blond hair
Thick like a wave
His eyes piercing, yet wet
The frame of one of those minor Olympians
Not over the top, just strong fitted
Mulling over the concept of not seeing another tomorrow
Fucker bawling like a baby looking into oblivion.
Not much in this place stands out
It's pretty much another drunken waste
Except- oh except- this is the last of the drinks
It's half past the hour, yet not quite nine
Doom starts at ten, a woman walks in
The one that carries uncertainty on her lips
She adorns the elegance of a lady
Yet wisdom of a snake
Her nature is of head games
Never ending drama
Just don't get close
She'll have a way of ripping things apart
Paying no mind to such uselessness
Cookie, just in different packaging
Back to it
Drinks and more drinks
In the end
Why not go out with style

Tripping Balls

One bar filled with people
A dire threat.
It's suddenly
End of the drinks

Gocni Schindler

Safe Place, it's Five AM

The phone chimes away
This comatose mind states
It's an earthquake?
Fuck this, L.A.
I reach into the dark
My hand, frantically flailing in the air
Smashing into the lamp
Banging the nightstand
Searching for the one said-
Noise making communication device
There is the piece of shit
I hear it
A voice cries out
Dear reader, understand
Have a little sympathy for me!
I'm now fucked that I hit the green
instead of the red
annoying voice blazes away

Are you there?

Ahh, fuck!

Oh, sorry, did I wake you?

No, not at all, it's only, what, five AM?

You serious, no huh, just your normal sarcastic self

What the hell do you want?

Oh, sorry, just needed to talk, totally not important

Tripping Balls

For the love of baby Jesus, it's obviously important

Ok, well, having a hard time here

Yeah, great, now what?

Need to find myself, I'm fat

Oh, how tragic

Serious, I don't feel important; men won't want me like this! Being fat in this town is a death sentence

Tragic, who said you were wanted?

That's not nice, thanks for that

Welcome

No, serious, I'm fat

Well, maybe you're not fat enough, ever think of that?

Why would you say that? You think I'm fat, knew it

Shit a loaf of bread, what do you think?

You're an asshole and not a safe place

Safe place, what, am I a house?

Meant, a place to come talk

Now I'm a support group, how great

Didn't mean it like that, just need a place I can come tell my issues, talk about them

Isn't that called a diary, don't you have some dumb box you'd call a friend, ya know, another female to call and talk to at 5 fucking AM?

Hate women, they're bitches, I should know

Wonderful, maybe that is part of the problem

I told you I was a lot to deal with

Well lucky fucking me, did I sign a waiver?

Whatever! Why are you being rude?

Oh, I don't know

Enter some fucked-up female noise

I'm so fat, don't know what to do, can't fit into my pants

Fuck me! Shit, meant, do you really think you're fat?

Oh, my god, seriously, like I'm a blimp, my pants don't fit

Shit, you're like a hundred pounds wet, how can this be?

My pants don't fit and I have to go to work

What the hell am I supposed to do?

What is your problem, I just need to talk!

Tripping Balls

Of course, you do

So, reader, at this point there is a series of silence, like eternity or something. Shit, I might have nodded off, who the hell knows? Then the voice comes back rudely

Aren't you going to say something?

Throw on some fucking yoga pants, is that all you needed, bills' in the mail

Why don't you listen to me?

Did I die, is this hell?

What does that mean, gosh, like, I never! Asshole!

This is what I'm talking about

What are you talking about?

This

Why did I even call you?

FUCK

Yes, reader, another series of silence, brutal it is, when all you want to do is sleep. Then the voice comes back after some heavy breathing and sighing

I called because...

After another moment of silence, this is that point where I needed to be a goddamn mind reader through the phone or something at 5 AM

Oh, let me guess, I'm supposed to know what you need?

Something like that would be nice, I want to be heard

Then go outside and scream

I'm serious

Yeah, you said that

Ugh, why do I call such an inconsiderate asshole?

That is a mystery you will need to figure out

I guess I don't think right

Maybe it would be best if you just stopped thinking

Do you think that would help?

Listen, you are nice and all but a bit too loopy for me

What the hell does that mean, too loopy?

It means, well it means, you are fucking crazy

That's not fair, I thought you were a safe place

I know how you can fit into your pants

How is that?

Tripping Balls

Jump off a rooftop into them

Click goes the phone
the world is dark
World, beautiful again
Silence
Time to go back to sleep
Farewell 5AM sanity test
Issued from the mentally insane

Gocni Schindler

I've walked a lonely road
What feels like millenniums
Upon shoeless toes

Tripping Balls

A BIG THANK YOU

Fuck yeah, you made it
Thanks for partaking
Hugs and kisses with a punch in the nuts
Get some cookies
Oreos made in the Mexicos
You know, they're number one
Purchase them, you can
Yes, you can, yes, you can, yes, you can
Acquire them at the local grocery store
Place them in mouth, chew, swallow
Just don't choke
Until we do it again, it's been fun
Peace out, you little freaks!

Gocni Schindler

Author Bio

Gocni Schindler is a bioluminescence of a singular human
A shadow amongst billions
Apart of the great humanity
Experienced, endured, suffered through, subsisted within worldly hell's
Written in this manuscript of man
Beholds a legend, protecting the guilty
Odd describes the childhood
Raised in a tavern
Rebellion the theme of the teen
A kid on fire
Looking for heaven
Virtuous in the twenties
Lost within thirties
Goals of forties
Survive
More to follow as the clock to his demise, tic toc's away
Gocni Schindler enjoys life
A character within his world
Delivering his heart to paper
It may be for you, might be for another
Regardless he believes you to be beautiful
Gocni Schindler creates, the end.

Tripping Balls

Other poetry titles from HellBound Books for your delectation...

DARK MUSINGS

Available at www.hellboundbookspublishing.com

Dark Musings by Xtina Marie

The perfect companion piece to Light Musings – The dark side of Xtina Marie's poetry delves into intense emotions: heartache, loss, hurt, pain, rage, and a dangerous consuming love which can drive one insane. Dark Musings is not a collection!

The author returned to the centuries old practice of Narrative Poetry—the telling of a story through poetry. If you believe you are brave enough to explore the savage emotions of the human heart; Dark Musings will test your mettle.

LIGHT MUSINGS

Available at www.hellboundbookspublishing.com

Light Musings by Xtina Marie

The perfect companion piece to Dark Musings – an intriguing mirror image of the darkness you have just read, but no less deep and soul stirring.

What a web she weaves. Light Musings is a poetic narrative—a story told through related poems. Xtina Marie is a master of this style. Known by her fans as the Dark Poet Princess, this term of endearment came about as a result of the horror genre embracing her first book: Dark Musings which continues to garner stellar reviews. Light Musings will not disappoint her loyal fans as darkness is present within these pages as well. However, this latest book will show a much larger audience that Xtina's poetry pulls out every feeling the reader has ever experienced—forcing them to feel with her protagonist. Light Musings shows us that love is made from darkness and light; something Xtina Marie explores like no one else.

A HellBound Books LLC Publication

www.hellboundbookspublishing.com

Made in the USA
Las Vegas, NV
27 June 2021